Catherine Cookson was born daughter of a poverty-stricken woman, Kate, whom she believed to be her older sister. She began working in service but eventually moved south to Hastings where she met and married a local grammar-school master. At the age of forty she began writing about the lives of the working-class people with whom she had grown up, using the place of her birth as the background to many of her novels.

Although originally acclaimed as a regional writer — her novel *The Round Tower* won the Winifred Holtby award for the best regional novel of 1968 — her readership soon began to spread throughout the world. Her novels have been translated into more than a dozen languages and more than fifty million copies of her books have been sold in Corgi alone. Thirteen of her novels have been made into successful television dramas, and more are planned.

Catherine Cookson's many bestselling novels have established her as one of the most popular of contemporary women novelists. After receiving an OBE in 1985, Catherine Cookson was created a Dame of the British Empire in 1993.

'Catherine Cookson's novels are about hardship, the intractability of life and of individuals, the struggle first to survive and next to make sense of one's survival. Humour, toughness, resolution and generosity are Cookson virtues, in a world which she often depicts as cold and violent. Her novels are weighted and driven by her own early experiences of illigitimacy and poverty. This is what gives them power. In the specialised world of women's popular fiction, Cookson has created her own territory.'
Helen Dunsmore, *The Times* (London)

The Lady on my Left

A NOVEL

CATHERINE COOKSON

CORGI BOOKS

LADY ON MY LEFT
A CORGI BOOK: 0 552 14569 6

Originally published in Great Britain by Bantam Press,
a division of Transworld Publishers Ltd

PRINTING HISTORY
Bantam Press edition published 1997
Corgi edition published 1999
Corgi Canada edition published 1999

Cover photograph John Alexander

Corgi Books are published by Transworld Publishers Ltd,
61-63 Uxbridge Road, London W5 5SA,
in Australia by Transworld Publishers (Australia) Pty Ltd,
15-25 Helles Avenue, Moorebank, NSW 2170,
and in New Zealand by Transworld Publishers (NZ) Ltd,
3 William Pickering Drive, Albany, Auckland.

Printed and bound in Canada

UNI 10 9 8 7 6 5 4 3 2 1

The Lady on My Left

One

THE AUCTIONEER PULLED IN HIS CHIN, PEERED over his spectacles, pushed his trilby hat up from his brow and said, 'What am I bid for this set of two-arm and four single Chippendale-design mahogany chairs? Splat backs, cabriole legs, claw and ball feet, they've got everything. Come along. Ten? All right, then, give me a start. Five . . . five it is . . . six . . . seven . . . eight . . . nine . . . ten . . . twelve. Did I hear fourteen?'

Alison Read pressed her long pencil to her lips and waited until the bidding reached £30 and then she joined in. At £34 there was only James Holbolt from High Bank left in against her and when, moving the pencil like a pendulum of a clock, she bid £38, Holbolt shook his head, which caused the auctioneer, with a machiavellian expression, to glance at Alison and say, 'A lady's bid. Thirty-eight pounds. A lady's bid.' This reference to 'a lady' was an auctioneer's trick to spur on an egotistical male from among the private buyers, but it didn't work on this occasion. The egotistical males grouped behind the chests of drawers and the oddments in the corner were all dealers and they knew Alison, knew for whom she was deputising.

'Going to the lady on my left. Any more? Any more, gentlemen?' The eyes roamed around the hall. Then the ivory hammer tapped gently on the desk. The auctioneer, glancing at his catalogues, then said simply, 'Aylmer.'

The clerk next to him went on writing, and then the next lot number was called, while Alison added £38 to her list of figures. She was glad she had got those chairs, having missed the Georgian set. They had been splendid – inlaid brass on turned legs – and Paul would have liked them. But still, she had got the French eight-day timepiece with the Sèvres plaques, and also the Georgian octagonal wine cooler. That was a really nice piece, with its mask-head handles and tapered legs. Unobtrusively, she edged out of her chair and crept around the back of the grouped bidders. As she passed the dealers, one whispered, 'How is Paul?'

Alison, also whispering, replied, 'Much better. I left him up and looking through catalogues.' They exchanged knowing smiles before she moved on, threading her way through the crowd to the outside door. Here she paused and pulled up the collar of her coat. The earlier snow had turned to sleet and at four o'clock on a late January afternoon it was almost dark. Because the roads were so treacherous, she hadn't brought the car; and as it was too cold to wait for a bus, she crossed the market square and took short-cuts through familiar narrow side streets and passages until, after ten minutes of brisk walking, she began to climb the short, steep hill of Tally's Rise, or as one wag had named the street, populated as it was almost entirely with antique shops, The Hill of Gold. And in many ways it *was* a hill of gold. Of the twenty-seven shops that lined each side of the street, fourteen sold old china and glass, or books, or antique furniture, and others a little of each. But this was not a street of junk shops. No knowledgeable person in the town went up Tally's Rise looking for junk. If they were able to buy a heavy decanter for 7s 6d, they could be sure it wouldn't be Georgian cut glass. But if they were looking for a pair of Georgian goblets with trumpet bowls and had a mind to pay in the region of £40 for them, then they had made a good buy. And they could find any amount of reproduction furniture in Tally's Rise, too, but not at what might be called bargain prices, for there was little shoddy stuff sold there. In the centre of the town you could buy a new oak chest of drawers for £10 and it would look grand. But for a chest not half as smart you would pay in the region of £50 in Tally's Rise – but then part of it might be Jacobean and it might have brass pear-drop handles. But even for that price you wouldn't get the real thing. The original, if you could find one, would cost anything from £300 to £500. Yes, it was a very interesting street, was Tally's Rise.

Aylmer's was the last shop at the top of the Rise. There was nothing beyond but a wall of rock. In fact, the rock – or the cliff-end, as it was – formed one wall of the basement shop and its doorway was the only access to the floors above.

Alison always said that as soon as she opened the shop door her world changed. Once through that door she found security, warmth and love, and never had her world been so welcome as it was on this bleak afternoon. She closed the door behind her and wiped her feet well on the doormat before stepping on to the drugget that made a straight pathway over the polished floor. On each side of her, set in skilful array, were pieces of furniture, all patina dark. Before she reached the end of the drugget, a man came through the doorway at the end of the long shop. He was an old man, with a patch over one eye, and shoulders so stooped as almost to form a hunch. But his smile was wide and his voice was cheery as he greeted Alison, 'By! you look frozen. Had they any heat on today?'

'About as usual, Nelson; I'm glad to get in.'

'Aa bet you are. Well, did you get anything? Did you get the mezzotints?'

'No, I'm sorry, Nelson, they went for a mint. But I got the clock with the plaques, you know, and also the chairs.'

'The Georgian lot?'

'No, I had to let them go. They made seventy-two pounds.'

'Whew! That was a price.'

'Have you done anything this afternoon?'

'No, Miss Alison.' He laughed. 'Not on a day like this.'

'No, of course not. They wouldn't get up this far, and I don't blame them. Have you had your tea?'

'No, not yet. Sweet Angeline will be bringing it any time now.'

Alison turned with a laugh from the old man, and opening a door on the right-hand side of the room, she stepped immediately into a thickly carpeted passage at the end of which a flight of stairs rose to the first floor. Here, on either side of a small landing, were two rooms, one her bedroom, the other Paul's. Another flight of thickly carpeted stairs brought her to a larger hallway and here she took off her coat and outdoor shoes. As she did so, a voice from the kitchen called, 'That you, Miss Alison? I bet you're glad to get in. What a day!' and a woman appeared in the hallway carrying a tray. She was short and stout, her face was covered with tiny wrinkles and her hair was black; although a questionable black. Her face assumed an expression of resentment as she said, 'I should make him come up for it.'

Alison said nothing, merely raised her eyes as she took her slippers out of the hall wardrobe. The feud that raged between Mrs Dickenson and Nelson was a source of amusement to Paul and herself. Nelson was from the North of England. Nellie Dickenson was a product of this small coast town, conservative and set in her ways, as she herself admitted, and Nelson's ready tongue and free manner irked her.

Edging her way on to the stairs, and balancing the tray on her hand, she said, 'It's all ready.'

'Thanks, Nellie.' Alison walked towards a door at the far end of the hall. Entering the drawing-room, she saw that it was indeed ready.

As usual, the tea-table was drawn up to the side of the huge fireplace, and sitting propped up on a couch before the fire, his large head resting on the back, was Paul Aylmer. Even sunk into the cushions as he was, he looked to be a big man. You could say at first glance that he was a Norwegian, with his thick fair hair streaked with grey at the sides. His face was big-boned, his eyes were wide apart but not deep-set, and they were topped by heavy brows. When his face was in repose the corners of his mouth were directed in an upward slant, giving his expression the appearance of amusement. Even when his eyes burned with deep anger the lips still kept their upward tilt, which was confusing to the onlooker. Altogether, it was a secret face, a quietly secret face, giving nothing away, and even when it did, it was likely to put you on the wrong track. But it was a face that represented Alison's world.

Alison was twelve years old when she first saw Paul Aylmer. Her Uncle Humphrey had often spoken of his wartime friend. Whenever he went south from Leeds to see him, he would leave her in the care of their housekeeper. On his return from one such visit, he said, 'Paul wants me to give up here and go into partnership with him, so I returned the compliment, as we are both in the same line. He likes the south coast, but I like good old Leeds and I can't see myself working anywhere else.'

A month later, she had met Paul Aylmer when he attended her Uncle Humphrey's funeral. She had come home from school one evening to find their housekeeper in floods of tears. Mrs Crosbie had said to her, 'Sit down, me dear; sit down and I'll tell you.' But even when she had heard the details she had difficulty in comprehending that her Uncle Humphrey was dead and that she was once more alone. Other people got pinned against walls by out-of-control lorries, but not her uncle. She couldn't remember her parents and her

Uncle Humphrey had been both mother and father to her. Her mother had died when she was two years old and her father had committed suicide soon after. She hadn't known about the suicide, though, until she was eleven years old, when she heard two men talking to her uncle in the shop. 'Tragic, that was,' one said, 'the mother dying and him not able to bear it. There's something to be said about restricting the ownership of firearms.'

After her uncle's funeral, the fact that she was now a wealthy little girl made little impression on her; what did was that her life and her affairs were entirely in the hands of her uncle's friend, Paul Aylmer. The big, quiet, fair man. And she also became aware, long before she left the solicitor's office, where gathered were her uncle's solicitor, their housekeeper, Paul Aylmer and herself, that her future guardian had been surprised to find himself with a ready-made daughter, as it were – and not altogether pleasantly surprised, either.

When they were alone together, she sat staring up at him, her wide dark eyes showing her loneliness and her fear of the future; her deep, inherent fear of being without folks . . . a family. And she was speechless with her fear. Then Paul Aylmer had smiled, and taking her hand, had said one word: 'Well?' It had broken through the spell of her fear and she had gabbled, 'I'll be no trouble. Uncle found me no trouble. I'll be very useful. I know a lot about furniture. Uncle taught me. I've been going to the sales for years; everyone knows me. I've even made bids.'

For the first time during their three days' acquaintance she saw him smile, and when she heard his laugh, deep and warm, and it rumbled around her, enfolded her, it drew her immediately out of herself and into him. From that moment she was lost and no part of her belonged to herself any more; it was as quick as that. He had said, 'I would hate to be called Father or Daddy,' and they had laughed again. 'My name's Paul. What about it?'

Paul, Paul, Paul. She had thought it the most wonderful name in the world. She still did. She went towards him now, saying, 'You know, you've worked it nicely, for it isn't fit for a dog to be out.'

The left-hand corner of his mouth moved further upwards. 'You've been trained well; you'll survive.'

'Cruelty.' She sat down near the table, and lifting the heavy silver teapot, began to pour out the tea, purposely keeping silent. And when she handed him his cup he nodded at her, saying, 'Well, out with it. How many snips did you get? Did you get the chairs?'

'Not the Georgian ones, but the Chippendale design, for thirty-eight pounds.'

He pursed his lips. 'Pity! I knew where I could place

that lot straight away at a hundred and thirty. Pity! Still, the Chippendale aren't bad. From what I saw of them they'll fetch sixty with a quick sale. Likely attract some young madam from the St Pierre section of the town.'

'But Paul, they're worth seventy at the least. If you start cutting so low you'll have old Broadbent on your tail again.'

'He's been on before and it hasn't made much impression.' They both laughed. Then reaching down to the foot of the couch he picked up a letter and handed it to her, saying casually, 'This is interesting.'

'What is it?'

'Read it and see.'

After Alison had read the letter she turned her eyes towards Paul and there was a note of excitement in her voice as she said, 'Beacon Ride. That's the enormous place standing back off the main Brighton road, isn't it?'

'Yes, that's the one.'

'And they want you to go there and value some pieces? Very nice, very nice, Mr Aylmer! It's a compliment, isn't it? They've passed over the three pushers, Broadbent, Fowler and Wheatley. Ah! That's what comes of having the name of an honest dealer attached to you! Yet ... yet, isn't it a bit odd ... Beacon Ride's close to Brighton. There're dozens of dealers, not to mention auctioneers and valuers in that quarter, and just by the law of averages, some are bound to be honest.'

Paul laughed again as he said 'Perhaps it isn't so strange after all; there's honesty and . . . honesty.'

'Don't be so smug.' Alison playfully punched him. Then looking sharply at the letter again she said, 'They ask you to go at your earliest convenience, but you won't be out of this house for another week or more.'

'Yes. Yes, I've thought of that, and we can't keep them waiting a week. When people want to sell they are usually in need of money.' He now rubbed the side of his nose with his finger as he murmured thoughtfully, 'I thought it was all gone, all the decent stuff . . . Odd.'

'How do you know? Have you been there before?' Her voice was pitched high.

Paul's eyes were cast down towards his plate as he remarked nonchalantly, 'Yes, a number of times.'

'When was this?'

'Oh . . . Oh, many many years ago, before you were born.' He slanted his gaze towards her and she smiled tenderly at him. The reference to her birth meant something that had happened before she came under his care eight years ago . . . She said now, 'Well, you don't want to lose this. What are you going to do?'

'I'm sending you.'

'Me? As a valuer?'

'Remember what you said to me the first day we came into partnership?' He pursed his lips on the word. 'You said you had been going to auctions for years. You said you knew . . . stuff.'

'Well, I did, and I do, don't I? But . . . this could be a big job. You've never let me go alone on anything like this before.'

'Nothing like this has cropped up before, so now's your chance. You'll go tomorrow.'

'Oh, Paul!' She leant towards him and grasped his hand. 'I'll love that, you know I will. What do you think it will be?'

'Well, it says in the letter there. Can't you read? Various pieces, including George the Third cutlery, Chinese porcelain, and some old English drinking glasses. It sounds interesting enough. What I can't understand is why they haven't sent them to London. Sotheby's would have been the people for that kind of stuff . . . if it is that kind of stuff.'

'Oh, lordy! I'm getting cold feet already.'

'Well, you needn't. All you've got to do is to list the items and work it out when you get back. You needn't state any price there, not if you feel in the least uncertain.'

'I'm shivering with excitement.'

She knelt down on the hearthrug, twisted her feet under her, and leant her back against the couch. Life was wonderful, excitingly glorious and wonderful.

She glanced towards the fire, wondering now, as she had done many times before, if she would have developed a taste for fine things, beautiful things, had her parents not died so tragically and had she not come under the care of her uncle. Her father had been nothing more exciting than a greengrocer. Perhaps if they had lived and she had grown up and married and had had a house of her own, the latent talent might have shown itself then. On the other hand, perhaps she had no innate talent in this direction. Perhaps it was merely the result of environment and chance, for her uncle had been extremely fond of her and had got into the habit of taking her to auctions with him whenever he could. As a child she had sat in corners in the old auction room in Leeds, surrounded by legs, while her uncle made his bids.

Her early dreams had been threaded by a voice saying, 'Going at ten shillings; going at twenty pounds; going at one hundred and fifty guineas. Going, going, gone.' She used to dance in the little backyard attached to the shop, skip and dance to a tune she made up and to lyrics that consisted solely of '*Going, going, gone.*' Anyway there was one thing certain, wonderfully certain: whether her knowledge was born of innate talent, or mere chance, she had it.

She was brought from her dreaming by Paul saying, 'I had a visitor this afternoon.'

'Yes?' She was still staring into the fire.

'Bill Tapley.'

'Oh, him. . . . I wondered why I didn't see him at the auction rooms.'

'He had more important business.'

'I can't imagine him thinking anything more important than making a deal, pushing somebody up.'

'He's a good businessman.'

'Good luck to him.'

'He wants to marry you.'

'What!' She shot round with the agility of a deer, and with her small, slim body, her elfin face, great dark eyes and mop of black hair she did resemble a startled animal, a frightened young animal. 'Bill Tapley wants to marry *me*? Are . . . are you serious?'

'*He* is.'

She bent forward and leant her elbows on his knees. Her face was below his now as she whispered, her voice laden with distaste, 'But he's well over forty! Bill Tapley! Him?'

'That's nothing against him.' Paul's lids were lowered. 'I'm on that way myself and I don't consider I'm in my dotage.'

She jerked her head back. 'You're only forty, you're only just forty. And anyway, he looks old enough to be your father.' She was exaggerating wildly and she knew it. She went on now, her nose wrinkled with distaste, 'But Bill Tapley! I never dreamed. . . . I don't like him.'

'I think he knows that.'

She sat back on her haunches. 'Then I'm glad, for I like nothing about him, his business ways least of all. And you're to blame there.' She nodded solemnly at him now. 'You shouldn't have brought me up to play fair. I've seen some of Bill Tapley's dealings with the Broadbent crowd . . . Marry him! Did he say so outright?'

'Yes, he did. He wanted my opinion on the matter.'

Her voice was very quiet when she asked, 'And what is your opinion on the matter?'

Again Paul was looking away from her. 'I said that it was entirely up to you. If you felt that way it was all right with me.'

She put her head on one side and surveyed him in astonished silence for a moment. 'You said that? You said that you would let me marry Bill Tapley?'

'Yes, if you wanted to.' He was looking down at her now. 'That is the main thing: if you . . . wanted . . . to.' He spaced out the last words.

'Well, I don't want to.' Her voice was loud, even shrill, and she turned from him and dropped on to her knees. 'I don't want to marry him or anyone else, and if it was a choice of dying alone or marrying Bill Tapley, I'd choose the former.' She jerked her head around to him. 'Do you know why Bill Tapley wants to marry me?'

'I think he's in love with you.'

'Don't be silly! Bill Tapley's in love with money. He knows that in seven months' time, when I'm twenty-one and free of my guardian,' she smiled gently at him, 'I'll have a tidy bit of cash: somewhere in the region of eighteen thousand pounds.'

'Much more than that. There's the interest, eight years of it.' Paul's voice was quiet.

'Well, eighteen thousand would be quite enough for Bill Tapley to get on with. Just let him ask me to marry him.' She nodded her head towards the fire, then swung round as Paul gave vent to one of his rare laughs. He was lying back on the couch shaking with his laughter, and now she bent over him, gripping him by the shoulders, trying in turn to shake his great frame. And then she too was laughing helplessly. But when her head dropped on to his chest just below his chin she felt the rumbling fade away as he became still. And after a moment, when she looked up, his face was straight and his eyes held that expression she didn't like, the one that shut her out. That was the only trouble with Paul, if she could call it trouble: one minute he was laughing and you thought he was as happy as a sandboy, the next he had that look in his eye which was always followed by silence.

She withdrew herself from him and rose to her feet, and sitting by the tea-table again, she refilled the cups, and as she drank she looked round the room, the room that she had created, the room which Paul had once described as a stolen world.

When she had first come to live in this house with Paul, the top floor had been divided into a sitting-room and a dining-room, with a conservatory leading off it. The conservatory was supported on a natural jut of rock, and from it you had a splendid view over tumbled roofs below and towards the sea. The rooms were furnished with pieces of good furniture, although all big Victorian stuff, and the whole had looked dull, everything forming a square. She had been seventeen when she left school and firmly determined to make the furniture trade her business, and so she had said to Paul, 'Let me start on the house. I could make it beautiful, I know I could.' So alive was her enthusiasm, so strong her conviction that the alterations she had in mind would transform the floors above the shop, that he fell in with her wishes, and part of the result was this, this lovely long room with the garden-room looking out towards the sea. The wall between the sitting-room and the dining-room had been demolished. The ugly partition that had screened off most of the conservatory had also disappeared. If there now arose a need to screen off the glass room it was done simply by closing the heavy magenta velvet curtains. The room itself was 38 feet long and 22 feet wide and covered the entire length of the shop and outbuildings. Covering the middle part of the floor at the drawing-room end was a Chinese washed carpet, with a smaller one at the dining-room end. Across the corner of the room at this end was no usual corner cabinet. Instead, there stood a Queen Anne bureau in walnut and sycamore, while in the opposite corner there was a William and Mary long-cased clock. This was also in walnut, with beautiful floral marquetry panels. Near one long window was placed a Georgian dining-table with chairs to match and, opposite it, against the far wall, stood a sideboard of the same period, its fluted tapered legs supporting bow-fronted cupboards. Most of the furniture at this end of the room was of the Georgian period. At the drawing-room end was a Bergère suite with acanthus, leaf carving and paw feet. This suite was upholstered in the same rich velvet that curtained the garden room. Flanking the alcoves at each side of the large white marble fireplace were a magnificent pair of Sheraton mahogany card tables and on each of them stood a wrought silver candlelabra. The plain grey mottled walls bore only three pictures, and these had been chosen for their colour rather than for their intrinsic value. One was a full-length portrait of a lady in blue brocade and lace with the simple title, 'The Frenchwoman.' The other two were flower studies. There were no expensive prints, which in spite of their value would merely have dulled this room. The walls held one other object and this was a column-sided Regency gilt mirror. It hung above the fireplace, although at the time of its installation there had been some protest from Paul, the only one in all her arranging. It was a foolish place to put a mirror, he said. He himself was sensible and didn't stand on the raised tiled fender to reach the mantelpiece, he said, but Alison was in the habit of doing this to give a last minute adjusting touch to her hat and never troubled about her skirt billowing towards the fire.

Indeed, the room was a stolen world, and no-one saw it without remarking on the unusualness of it.

Alison looked round it now. 'Marry Bill Tapley and leave this!' Her shoulders hunched just the slightest with the inward 'Huh!' she gave. Then her eyes dropped to Paul Aylmer's profile. Marry Bill Tapley and leave all this? Her eyes remained fixed on him as she repeated to herself: And leave all this?

Two

AT ELEVEN O'CLOCK THE FOLLOWING MORNING Alison turned the car slowly from the slushy main road into the dark tree-lined drive that led to Beacon Ride. About a quarter of a mile along the road she had caught sight of the house across the park, the bare branches of the trees scratching a pattern across the vast flat-faced façade. The drive seemed to wind away from the house before swinging in its direction again, and along its whole length it was bordered by stark intertwined trees. Although leafless, they made a dark tunnel, and when at last she emerged from it there in front of her stood the house. And her aesthetic feeling was numbed by the sight of it. Nowhere was it protectingly covered with any kind of creeper that lends charm to old houses and often hides their scars. Here the scars were naked to the eye; great patches of peeling stucco, a whole length of guttering slanting drunkenly from one corner, and the pointing on the wall at this corner deeply eroded. Once it must have looked a mighty, dignified dwelling. Now it looked senile.

Alison drew the car to a stop at the foot of the broad steps leading up to the front door. The condition of the house, she thought, was likely the reason for her visit today. Money was needed badly here, that was evident. But it would take a great deal of furniture, glass and porcelain to repair even the façade of this great place. It was a nice little horde of jewels that was wanted here. She smiled wryly to herself as she slowly mounted the steps. Say a diamond tiara, two or three old necklaces and a dozen rings or so, just to start with. If it was big money they were after then it should be, as Paul had said, someone from Christie's or Sotheby's who should be about to knock on this front door. Although Paul's business was very good, their main sales were in a range of £10 up to £100, occasionally reaching the £200 mark, but it would take thousands, even tens of thousands, to put this place on its feet.

She was full of curiosity as her finger pressed the bell. She had to wait some time before the door was opened, and then she was confronted by an old woman with a sparse figure and a long, lined face below a mass of white hair. She was small, no more than five feet three or four inches, so her eyes were almost on a level with Alison's. And when she spoke her voice had a high, refined note. 'Yes, you were wanting . . . ?' She waited.

'I've come in Mr Aylmer's place. He is indisposed at the moment with flu.' She held out the letter for the woman to see. 'I've an appointment with Mrs Gordon-Platt. Mr Aylmer phoned last night.'

'Oh?' The old woman seemed to hesitate. Her head went to one side and then she asked, 'Which Mrs Gordon-Platt? Mrs Charles?'

'I don't know. I only know it's Mrs Gordon-Platt.'

The troubled look deepened on the woman's face, then she turned from Alison and said, 'Well, you'd better come in.'

Alison followed the thin, stooped figure across the huge dim hall. Her eyes searched quietly, as was her business, for the period pieces that delight all dealers, but they found nothing interesting. There was furniture in the hall, but it was late Victorian stuff, large and ornate, and very ugly.

'What's your name?' The old woman paused with her hand on the handle of a door.

'Alison Read. Miss Alison Read.'

The next moment Alison was standing behind the old woman in the doorway of a drawing-room, and from where she stood she saw another woman sitting writing at a table drawn up close to the fire. She saw her turn her head towards the doorway, then swing round and say, 'What is it, Beck?'

'This young lady says she has an appointment with Mrs Gordon-Platt.'

'Appointment?' The woman had risen to her feet and was staring at Alison. 'I've made no appointment with you.'

'I've come in place of Mr Paul Aylmer. It was to value some glass and china.'

She watched the woman's hands go quickly to her neck, the fingers pressing gently on the windpipe. She watched her swallow before turning round and saying, 'Oh, yes. Yes, now I understand. Come in. I did write to Mr Aylmer. That will be all, Beck.'

As Alison went to move forward she glanced at the old woman, who was staring at the back of the tall Mrs Gordon-Platt. She watched her lower her head and bite on her lip before turning away. Then the door was closed, and she walked towards the fire. And the attitude of the woman who stood awaiting her caused her to ask, 'You *are* Mrs Gordon-Platt?'

'Ye . . . es. I'm Mrs Gordon-Platt.'

'You were expecting me?'

The tall woman smiled now, and gave a slight laugh as she said, 'Well, not really.'

'But you wrote to Mr Aylmer, asking for some things to be valued.'

'Yes. Yes, I did.'

'And he phoned you last night to say I was coming.'

Alison watched the eyes flit downwards. The smile had vanished from the woman's face. She saw her glance sharply towards the ceiling before saying, 'Oh. I can see where the mistake has occurred. I'm Mrs Gordon-Platt Junior, Mrs Charles. Mr Aylmer must have spoken to my mother-in-law. But do sit down.' She motioned Alison to a seat. 'This is going to be slightly awkward. I must explain. You see, my mother-in-law is very old and . . . well—'. There was a smile on the face again, and it was a bit too smarmy for Alison's liking. 'She is incapable of making decisions. My son manages the estate and I see to the household. And . . . and things are rather tight at present, so we decided to dispose of some glass and silver . . . By the way, how is Mr Aylmer?'

'He has flu.' Alison moved her head forward. 'Do you know him?'

The lids drooped yet again, and her face was once more wreathed in a smile. 'Yes. Yes, I know Mr Alymer. It is some years now since we met, but I knew him very well at one time. May I ask if you are his niece? You can't be his daughter, as I understand he isn't married.'

For a moment Alison didn't answer: she was looking at this woman with new interest. She was the type that could wear a sack and yet appear smartly dressed. She was wearing a plain blue-wool dress without any attending ornament. She did not even wear a wedding ring, and her hair, which was fair and not unlike the colour of Paul's, was lifted straight back from her forehead. She was an imposing looking woman. She might be anything between thirty-five and forty, yet she could also pass for thirty. A strange uneasiness had been filtering into Alison as she summed up Mrs Gordon-Platt, and her voice betrayed this with a stiffness, as she replied, 'No, I am not his niece, I am his ward.'

'Ward? Really, you surprise me, I couldn't imagine Paul having the patience to bring up a child. Is he still as taciturn and grumpy?'

The uneasiness was deepening but whatever answer Alison might have made to this was checked by the drawing-room door being thrust open with such force that it banged against the wall. Both she and the woman swung round, and her own mouth dropped into a gape when she saw the grotesque and almost frightening figure of an old lady. She was fat, enormously so, and this was exaggerated by the amount of clothes she was wearing, for underneath a voluminous dressing-gown there showed a nightdress, and around her shoulders were draped at least two shawls and a scarf. But it was her head that was the most startling. This was bare of any covering other than hair which could not possibly have been real, for the woman in the doorway must have been eighty if she was a day and her hair was a startling mass of a bright auburn colour.

'So, so!' The voice was as big as the body. 'Am I interrupting anything?' She took a few steps into the room. They were slow and unsteady, giving the lie to the strength that her size and voice suggested.

Alison turned swiftly to the younger Mrs Gordon-Platt, and she noticed that her expression was a mixture of defiance and hate, and that these emotions looked frozen into the whiteness of her skin.

Now there appeared from behind the voluminous skirts of the old lady the figure of Miss Beck. She was making a motion with her hands as if she were clapping them gently, and her voice had a whimpering sound as she said, 'Oh, madam . . . madam . . . please come . . . come away back to bed. You'll make yourself ill. Oh, please, madam.'

'Quiet! Beck. I won't make myself ill. I'm never ill; I just imagine I am. Isn't that so, Freda?' The small pale eyes seemed to be squirting jets of red light on to her daughter-in-law, and when she received no answer she laughed. In contrast to her age and size, the laugh was young and had a quaint, tinkling sound. And then she turned to Alison and said abruptly, 'You're the young person Mr Aylmer has sent?'

All Alison could do was to incline her head. For the moment she was speechless and continued to be so as the old lady went on, 'I did not tell Mr Aylmer last night when he was on the phone that it was not I who had written to him; also that if I wished to dispose of any of my property there is a firm in Brighton which has served me very well in the past. I wanted to get to the bottom of this. If I had prevented you from coming and spoken about the matter to my daughter-in-law' – the eyes flashed towards the pale woman – 'she would, with her usual duplicity, have been able to wriggle out of the situation. So I thought I would let it come to a head . . . Sit down.' She pointed an imperious finger at Alison, and Alison, as if she had been prodded with a long pole, sat down. Then, doddering forward like a top-heavy old battleship, the old woman shuffled to the fireplace, with Beck spluttering at her side. After lowering herself slowly on to an upright chair, she turned to her daughter-in-law and said sharply, 'I'm waiting.'

The tall, pale woman, speaking through lips that barely moved, now answered, 'It can't go on for ever.' She said these words slowly and they seemed to make little impression on the old woman, but Beck gasped in horror as she looked towards her mistress's daughter-in-law and murmured reproachfully, 'Oh, how could you, Mrs Charles.'

'She could all right, Becky, don't let it worry you.'

The old head was shaking. 'But I'll not die just to spite her.' She flung the words towards the stiff back that moved now, with what Alison grudgingly admitted was an example of quiet dignity, towards the drawing-room door. And when it was closed, and this done quietly also, the old lady gave the whole of her terrifying and scrutinising attention to Alison, and Alison sat under it like a hypnotised rabbit for some minutes until Mrs Gordon-Platt's voice broke the spell, saying, 'What do *you* know about good silver or glass, or anything else in this category, for that matter? You are still a child. He had a nerve to send you.'

'Nothing of the sort.' The spell was broken and the tone of her voice surprised even Alison herself. 'I was brought up in the business. Mr Aylmer wouldn't have sent me here unless he felt I was sufficiently experienced to value your property.'

The muscles of the old face worked vigorously for a moment before she said, 'Well, whatever your quali-fications, you have made your journey for nothing. My daughter-in-law owns nothing in this house, and she hasn't the power to sell a button. Yet . . . yet she has been doing it, hasn't she, Beck?' As she asked this question she turned to her maid with a pathos that was in absolute contradiction to her manner of a few moments before. She was now like a child seeking protection from its mother, and Beck was the mother.

The maid lifted up the wrinkled, bejewelled hand, saying, 'Yes, madam; no-one has any legal right to anything in the house except yourself. It's all yours.'

Alison saw the other wrinkled hand tap Beck's in a gesture of thanks. Then turning her attention to Alison again, the old lady said, 'My daughter-in-law is a thieving, scheming she-cat,' and her head had bounced with the words. It would seem that she was well back in her stride, and Alison dared to ask, quietly, 'Then why do you live together?'

The old head jerked up so quickly that Alison had to suppress a smile when the neat pile of hair moved slightly. 'You are an impertinent young woman,' she was told.

'Madam, she was only—'

'Yes, yes, I know, Beck. Be quiet! And don't tell me I've asked for what I'm getting. I know. I know. All right.' She now bowed deeply towards Alison and went on in a maudlin way: 'You ask why my daughter-in-law and I live together. Well, I'll tell you. It doesn't matter now; everyone knows . . . When my son married that woman twenty years ago I turned him out and I haven't seen him from that day to this.' Her voice trembled as she continued, 'And I won't see him now, for he died two years ago.'

Alison was silent, and Beck, patting her mistress's shoulder, said, 'There, now. There, now. Don't distress yourself.'

'And my husband was a fool, a kindly fool, so what did he do when he died last year but leave everything to his grandson, provided that he came and lived here. And so he came; but he had been brought up by his dear mama and wouldn't stay without her. What can I do?' She spread her arms wide and then gave a little senile chuckle as she added, 'But what a surprise that madam got, for the inheritance is a mortgage that would throttle the Bank of England. They can't sell the land until I'm gone, and even with the fancy prices they are getting today it wouldn't meet the debts anyway.' Again came the senile chuckle. 'And then you know, my dear' – the old lady's manner changed again and she clutched at Alison's hands and began talking as if to a dear friend – 'look what they did when I was in hospital. They only sent me there because they were so sure I'd never come out again. But I did, didn't I?' Without waiting for Alison to answer she went on, her voice now breaking into a sob, 'They were so sure I was going to die they stripped my room. They sold my cabinets . . . Oh, my cabinets.' The auburn hair bounced gently on the nodding head. 'But it wasn't the cabinets, it was what was inside them, wasn't it, Becky?'

As Beck answered by patting the old lady and murmuring soothing endearments, Mrs Gordon-Platt's attitude changed yet again and, her eyes narrowing, she exclaimed, 'You say you are a dealer?'

'Yes.'

'You get about, then?'

'Yes. Yes, I do.'

'You go to all the sales?'

'No. No, just the ones where we think there'll be useful pieces, the kind of pieces we sell.'

'You might have seen my cabinets, then. Oh, my cabinets.' The face was awash with tears, and Beck, her face also crinkling, murmured, 'Now, madam, you'll only upset yourself. And you can't do anything about it. Come along. Come along.'

'Yes; yes, it's too late to worry. I'm tired, Beck. This has been too much. Give me your arm.'

It was as much as the maid could do to get the old woman to her feet, but when Alison went hastily to her assistance she was rebuffed quietly but firmly. 'It's all right, miss, I can manage. Madam is all right.'

Helplessly, Alison stood watching the two women shambling from the room, and it was hard to tell who was leaning on whom.

What was she to do now? Go home, she supposed. She looked round the great ugly room. Oh, it was pitiable that families such as these should end in this way. She loved old houses. She loved old families. Her eyes fell on a high-backed chair upholstered in velvet, with the overall colour being a dark grey, although the corners gave evidence that it had once been red. As she stared at the chair an odd feeling of recognition spread through her . . . She knew that chair; she had seen it before. Her commonsense told her she was being silly, and she asked herself how she could possibly have seen it when she had not been in this house before. And yet, she knew she had seen it . . .

She looked towards the open door through which the two elderly women had passed and realised she had seen them before too. But then she thought, Come on, get out of this place. You're light-headed . . . or going around the bend. You couldn't possibly have seen them before . . . or that chair.

No, of course she couldn't. They had both made such a strong impression on her in the last few minutes, more of an impression than some people would make in a lifetime, that it had given her the idea she had met them before . . . that was it. But did she have the same feeling about the younger Mrs Gordon-Platt? No. No, she had no feeling that she had met *her* before. But she did have the feeling that she didn't want to see her again. And this feeling was strong.

She picked up her bag and gloves from the floor, cast one look at the high-backed chair and turned about, intending to march briskly from the room and the house, but there in the doorway, standing quietly and gazing at her, was a young man.

'Hello,' he said and smiled.

She did not answer him but looked him up and down. He was about her own age, or perhaps younger.

She had no need to ask herself who he could be. This was the heir to the mortgage, all right. And although he was clearly his mother's son, he had a pleasant face.

'Are you waiting for someone?'

'No. I was just leaving.'

He did not move to let her pass. 'You came to see my mother?'

'Yes, I came to see your mother.' Her voice was curt. 'And I've seen her; also your grandmother.'

'Oh Lord!'

Her manner towards him changed abruptly as she watched him close his eyes and droop his head in boyish dismay. 'That would be something to see. They were together in the same room?'

'Yes.' Her voice held a hint of laughter now. 'Your grandmother made the journey downstairs.'

Again he said, 'Oh, Lord!' and then moving aside as if to let her pass he asked, 'What was your business?'

'I was given to understand that I was to value some glass and silver.'

Now his face showed concern as he asked, 'At whose request?'

'Your mother's, I understand. It is a bit confusing having two Mrs Gordon-Platts.'

'Yes . . . yes.' He nodded his head and although he was staring at her she realised that his thoughts were not on her. She was given to making snap decisions and to quick likes and dislikes. She knew that she disliked the younger Mrs Gordon-Platt and she pitied the elder. She also knew that she could like Mr Gordon-Platt. He was merely a boy, yet already he was loaded with responsibility. She wondered how he would stand up to it. He was pleasant, but not too strong, she thought; there was nothing firm or mannish about him. She had a mental picture of Paul. She said quickly, 'Goodbye.'

'Wait a minute. May I ask your name?'

'Alison Read.'

'You live nearby?'

'Not far.' She smiled, and he answered it, then asked on a laugh, 'Is that your car outside?

'Yes.'

'It's nice. I like Rovers. You can't go wrong with them.'

'That's what I think too.' They walked together through the hall and down the steps, silent now and both awkward. He opened the car door for her and not until she was at the wheel did he speak again. And then he smiled quizzically at her as he said, 'Pity we can't do business with you.'

'Yes.' She laughed now. 'It is.'

'You don't look like a dealer.'

'You should never go by appearances.' She found it easy to banter with him. Suddenly she was sorry for him. He was entirely out of keeping with this house. Symbolically, it was like a large tombstone balancing precariously above him and when his grandmother died it would fall on him, and from the look of him she did not think he would be able to withstand its weight. She had the strange urge to make him feel happy. She was concerned for him as if he were a brother. That was the daft part about her, she told herself. She was forever forming people she liked into close relationships with herself. They were either brothers or sisters, or fathers, or aunts, or uncles, but . . . but never husbands. She said now, 'If you unearth any bags of diamonds from behind the secret panels, give me a ring. We're Aylmers of Tally's Rise, in Sealock.'

'I will. That's a promise. You can be sure I will.' They laughed together like old friends, and then she was away, down the drive towards the main road.

He was a nice boy. She thought of him as a boy. But what a set-up to live in. Poor soul. She paused before entering the main road, then seeing the road clear she swung to the left, only to apply the brakes as a hand came out from a parked car and waved at her to stop. After pulling into the side of the road she assumed a stiff expression and watched Bill Tapley crossing towards her.

'Hello, there, you haven't been long after all.' He leant his hands on the window frame.

'What do you mean, haven't been long?' She looked at him coldly.

'Well, I expected you to be there for a couple of

hours.' He grinned at her. 'They're on the sell again, aren't they?'

'Since you know, why do you bother to ask? And why put yourself to the trouble of waiting for me?'

As soon as she had said this she regretted it, for she had given him a lead.

He now put his head in through the open window, 'Paul say anything to you about me last night?'

She edged back along the seat to get away from the close proximity of his face and lied glibly, saying, 'No, why should he?'

'Oh.' He moved his head in small jerks, then looked down at his hand where it rested on the frame, before saying, 'I somehow thought he might.'

'Look, I'm in a hurry, I want to get back. Moreover, I'm in need of my lunch.'

'That can soon be rectified. Come and eat it with me.'

'No, thanks.'

'Paul did say something about me last night, didn't he? He told you why I popped round to see him yesterday... Why don't you give me a chance, Alison?'

'Chance!' She screwed up her face at him, and at this his pleasant expression vanished and he said stiffly, 'Come off it. Don't play the sophisticated miss. It doesn't suit you. You might have gatecrashed into the male world but you're still Little Miss Demure

under it all ... and a bit of a prig too, aren't you?
... Oh, for God's sake!' – He wagged his head in
desperation – 'There I go putting my foot into it again.
I always get off on the wrong foot with you. I'm a fool
... Look, Alison, the fact is I've had you in mind for
a long time and I want you and me to get pally. If
Paul didn't tell you last night then I will now.' He
laughed at her and again shook his head. 'It's a funny
place to propose with my head sticking through the
car window ... Move over.' He withdrew his head
and made as if to open the door, when Alison said
abruptly, 'No, no! I can give you your answer now.
It's ... it's no.' She had to bend forward to look up at
him for he was now standing straight, his thick body
spreading beyond each side of the car window. And
although she disliked him, she felt she must soften the
blow, so she added, 'Your interest in me has come as
a surprise.'

'That's a lie. You've always known I've had a
liking for you.' His round, plain face had a stiff, dull
expression about it, yet he smiled as, bending down
to her once more, he said, 'This is only the beginning.
I don't give up easily. Do you know, I've been as far as
Edinburgh in the depth of winter after some little thing
I was interested in? Little things are often precious. I
appreciate this fact and am prepared to work hard to
get them, understand?' She did not answer, and so he
said, 'Well, you can go on your way; I won't detain

you any longer. Only tell Paul I proposed and was rejected, will you? See what he says.'

She stared at him for a moment before re-starting the engine, letting out the clutch and accelerating away. What did he mean, tell Paul and see what he says? It was a funny thing to say and he had said it in a funny manner; she was disturbed by it. Oh, what a morning! She wished she were home.

As she entered the shop, Nelson was vigorously polishing the top of a Welsh dresser, and he turned to her, saying without any preamble, 'It's been a good mornin'. I've sold the tub armchair, the one in the blue silk damask. An' the Sutherland table. An' the four-tier what-not. I asked fifteen for that . . .'

'But it was only marked at twelve!'

'Aye, I know, but she was one of these wives who gets a kick out of a bargain. You know I can tell them a mile off. So her and me had a nice half-hour. When I asked her fifteen she acted as if she was goin' to have a fit. But I knew by the gleam in her eye she was ready to bite, so we had a nice little game. She beat me down to thirteen pounds-ten. What do you think of that?'

Alison bit on her lip, then burst out laughing. 'You are the limit, Nelson! You know he doesn't like it, don't you?'

She indicated the upstairs rooms with a lift of her

head, and to this Nelson replied, 'He'd be better off than he is the day if he stuck out for a bit more.' He stabbed his finger towards her. 'An' if he didn't let you have all them choice pieces for them rooms up there. Bit soft in the head that way, he is, I think.' His harsh words were accompanied by a twisted smile and she turned from him, still laughing, and went upstairs.

When she entered the drawing-room Paul, fully dressed, was standing in the archway to the garden-room. He had been gazing out towards the sea but turned swiftly to meet her, asking, 'Well, how did it go?'

'It didn't.'

'What do you mean? You didn't state a price and shake them, did you?' His tone held an unusual note of criticism, to which she replied swiftly, 'No. No, I didn't. I didn't get a chance. Let me get my things off and I'll tell you . . . How are you feeling?' She turned an eager face towards him, but he shook his head, saying, 'I'm all right. But go on, tell me what happened.'

So, sitting herself down in an armchair to the side of the fireplace, she went over the whole procedure from the beginning, omitting only Mrs Gordon-Platt Junior's interest in him. She did not ask herself why she was withholding this, but she knew that if she were to mention it at this point it would be crowded out by other things and would lose its significance; perhaps give him the opportunity to pass it over without any explanation at all. She didn't want that. Of all the things that had happened that morning, she wanted one thing made clear: how well had he known Mrs Gordon-Platt all those years ago? Because some part of her was worried with the knowledge that they had at one time been acquainted. But by the time she reached the episode concerning Bill Tapley's proposal, she saw, with some annoyance, that Paul's attention had gone from her. He was sitting with his legs crossed and his elbow on his knee, systematically biting around the top of his thumbnail. She said sharply, 'Did you hear what I said, Paul? Bill Tapley told me to tell you that he had proposed.'

'What?' He uncrossed his legs and sat upright. 'Oh . . . Bill Tapley. What did he say?'

She said slowly, 'He told me to tell you that he had asked me to marry him and . . . asked what had you to say about my refusal.'

'Oh, he did, did he? And you refused him. Why?'

'Don't be silly, Paul. What's the matter with you? I told you last night. I also told you why he wants me.'

Paul was once more standing in the archway looking towards the sea and he didn't answer her for some seconds, and then he said, 'You say you saw the younger Mrs Gordon-Platt?'

She stood up and stared at his broad back, and

after a moment she answered flatly, 'You know I did. I told you everything that happened.' And now she put her question. 'How friendly were you and Mrs Gordon-Platt years ago, Paul?'

The silence was heavy on the room. It was as if he hadn't heard her; although he had, and when he answered, his voice was quite even. 'Well enough to be engaged to marry.' When he turned to her, the corner of his mouth indicated some amusement, and he said, 'Stop gaping. You look like a flat fish.'

Alison closed her mouth and swallowed. She had just received a shock that was making her heart race. All of a sudden she was frightened. Quite plainly she could see the pale woman sitting writing at the table near the fire in that cold drawing-room, and she realised now that the picture had about it a certain appeal, even to her. What effect would it have had on a man to see a widow, lonely, trying to manage that great place with the help of a mere boy. Mrs Gordon-Platt had wanted to see Paul for a purpose, and Alison now thought she knew that purpose, and it wasn't concerned with the sale of any silver or glass. As the old lady had said, there were other auctioneers and valuers. Why, if they had been selling stuff for the last year or so, hadn't they contacted Paul before?

Alison felt a desperate urge to fling herself on Paul and cry, 'You'll not go and see her, will you? You won't take up with her again, will you?' She could see the woman standing beside Paul, the same height, the same age, with similar ideas because of a similar generation . . . Definitely similar ideas. If they had been close enough at one time to almost marry . . . She suddenly felt sick.

'Come on.' He dug her gently in the shoulder. 'Come on, have some lunch; you look both cold and hungry. I'll give Nellie a shout.'

'I don't feel like any lunch.'

'Whether you feel like it or not you're going to eat it and I refuse to talk about anything until you have.' He pulled a face at her. 'That should give you an appetite, Miss Read, if nothing else will. Your curiosity will choke you if it is not appeased soon, won't it?'

Oh, you!' She rushed at him and hung on to his arm and laughed now in spite of herself. But at the same time a part of her was crying in a desperate way, Oh, dear God, don't let anything happen to disrupt our way of life together.

Lunch over, Mrs Dickenson brought in the coffee and as she placed it on the side table she stated flatly, 'That Nelson says he's got to go out and fetch them things from the auction room and would you take over, Miss Alison?'

It was some seconds before Alison replied, 'All right, Nellie, tell him I'll be down right away.'

No sooner had the door closed on Mrs Dickenson

than Paul, dropping on to the couch, began to chuckle; then, shaking his head towards Alison standing there surveying him, he laughed outright as he said, 'Fate is against you, my little inquisitor. We were to settle down and have a glorious rake into the past, weren't we? . . . and then old Nelson puts his spoke in.' The laughter subsided into a rumbling chuckle as he went on, 'Being the wise miss that you are, you know that an opportunity lost is never regained, and it will be more difficult to get anything out of me after the iron has cooled, so to speak, and after a couple of hours in the shop. How on earth will you lead up to it?'

Swiftly Alison picked up a cushion and heaved it at him. It missed his head but knocked his pipe out of his hand. The pipe bounced off the coffee table on to the tiled hearth. There was a gentle snapping sound and the bowl was severed from the stem.

'Oh, I'm sorry.' Alison was all contrition now. She held the two pieces in her palm and looked at them, and Paul looked at them, his face solemn. Yet the fixed corner of his mouth belied his tone as he said, 'I liked that pipe; you get used to a pipe. Pipes are like people; you don't want to part with them.'

Taking his words seriously, she said, 'I know . . . I know.' Her lips began to tremble and her head was drooping, when suddenly her hands were grasped firmly and she was pulled down to the couch, and Paul, shaking her gently, said, 'Don't be a silly little clot. What is a pipe? Now stop it. What's come over you? . . . Look' – he put his finger under her chin – 'Look at me. Are you worrying about something?'

She shook her head and blinked in an effort to keep the tears back.

'Well, what's the matter, then?' Without waiting for a reply he gave her the answer, saying, 'Now look here. Forget everything that happened at that house this morning. It's a pity I sent you there. I wouldn't have done, but I thought the letter was from . . . well . . . Freda and Florence both begin with an F . . . that was my mistake.' He gave a toss of his head. 'Let's finish it. No more talk of Beacon Ride or its inhabitants. They are all in the past, and the past is dead and buried.' He pressed with his finger and lifted her chin further. 'I mean that. And also' – his voice sank low – 'I'm going to ask you not to mention it again. I'll do no business with the Gordon-Platts. I must have been mad even to think about it. There it is. As I said, it's the past, and I don't want it revived. Understand?' His eyes were holding hers, but she made no response. She didn't understand. The very fact that he had been disturbed to learn that Mrs Freda Gordon-Platt was now living at Beacon Ride, and then had made light of the whole thing, proved to her that the business went deeper than he would have her believe. Of course it went deep. If he had almost married her it was bound to

51

have gone deep. Added to which, that he now wanted to close the matter finally did nothing to lessen the strange anxiety that was filling her. But Paul, taking her silence for assent, nodded at her as he said, 'Well, that's that. Now let's have coffee, then go and relieve Nelson, that's a good girl.'

'Oh, don't call me a good girl. You stopped doing that years ago.'

His eyes widened while they remained fixed on her, and now he pursed his lips and said with mock sternness, 'Very well, Miss Read . . . You little stinker! with a temper like a vixen. Take your coffee, get out of my sight and go and relieve Nelson, for if he doesn't get that stuff moved they'll start filling up the sale room again and pushing it around, and we'll have it chipped top, bottom, middle and sides. That's assuming the pieces weren't all stuck with glue when you bought them. Likely they'll drop to bits when he tries to load them.'

She knew she was being ribbed, but she made no attempt to retaliate. She did not want to be jocular, she did not feel jocular and she suspected Paul's manner was merely a cover for something . . . something, but what? She remembered the expression on his face when she told him she had found two Mrs Gordon-Platts at Beacon Ride. He had been startled, jolted, and he hadn't been quick enough to hide his reactions to this news.

She picked up her cup of coffee and left the room without saying goodbye. When she reached the shop Nelson said, 'Sorry, Miss Alison, but Aa thought you might have forgotten and planned to go out, like. You know what it is if they start bringing fresh stuff into the rooms—our stuff gets pushed to the back.'

'Yes. Yes, it's all right, Nelson, I hadn't forgotten.'

'Aa'll go and get me coat. Will Aa take the cheque or will you see to it?'

'I dropped it in this morning when I was passing.'

'Oh, good.'

Nelson went into the back room to get his coat, and Alison placed her cup of coffee carefully on a pad that rested on a Chippendale tray-top wine table. She looked about her, then decided she would polish the Empire escritoire, take the drawers out and give them a good clean. She was lifting the box of dusters from a cupboard when the bell tinkled as the shop door opened and, raising her head above the level of the cupboard to see who had entered, she remained stationary in a bent, half-crouching position as she exclaimed, 'No! Oh no!' The woman was now moving towards her.

'Good afternoon. No doubt you are surprised to see me again so soon. I've called to see Mr Aylmer.'

'He's . . . he's not well. I told you this morning. He's got flu.'

'I'm not afraid of germs.' The lips moved into a cool

smile. 'Perhaps you will tell him I'm here, and ask if I could see him. I won't stay long, I promise you.'

'Well, here I am, miss, all ready to—' Nelson stopped and stared at the woman, and from her to Alison, and then back to the woman again. And he remained staring at her even when Alison said, 'Will you wait a minute or two, Nelson? I'm going upstairs.' She did not look at the woman again but went stiffly across the shop and through the door. Then she seemed to fly up the two flights of stairs and she was gasping as she thrust open the drawing-room door.

Paul's head turned towards her in surprise as she closed the door, and then without moving from it she hissed, 'She's downstairs.'

'Who's downstairs?' He swivelled round on the couch.

'Mrs Gordon-Platt. Mrs Charles Gordon-Platt. She wants to see you.'

He was on his feet as if he had been kicked with a spiked stirrup, and he stared at Alison for a full moment before, his eyes moving from her, he said, 'I can't see her now. Tell her I'm not well; I've got flu.'

'I've already told her that. But I'll tell her again. Perhaps she'll believe me this time.'

She had opened the door and was almost in the hall when his voice halted her. 'Wait! Wait a minute. Come here. Close the door.' She did as she was bidden and stood waiting for him to speak again. Her heart was racing painfully. And she was filled once more with that strange fear of impending loss and loneliness attending the loss. Paul was standing with his shoulders and head bent now, and it was from this position that he said, 'Send her up.'

'But Paul!'

'Alison!' He lifted his head but did not straighten his back as he looked at her, and his tone was one that would brook no argument. She had heard it once or twice before. 'Send Mrs Gordon-Platt up.'

Without another word she turned from him and went down the stairs and into the shop.

Mrs Gordon-Platt was examining a French carved, threefold, dwarf screen with panels painted after the manner of Vernis Martin. She brought her glance from it as Alison spoke. 'He will see you for a few minutes.'

'Thank you.' A smile slid from the lips up over the face, and as she came forward she said, 'You have a lot of nice pieces here. That's a lovely little screen.'

Alison made no comment, but led the way through the door and up the stairs. And when she reached the hallway her heart was beating so loudly the sound was reverberating through her head. She hadn't felt like this since the day the housekeeper had told her her Uncle Humphrey had died. She opened the door and made way for the woman to pass her, and then she was looking at Paul, who was looking at the woman. He was standing opposite the door waiting for her. Alison watched the woman pause and gaze across the distance towards him. She saw her face soften and a smile take up each feature. It was a different face from the one she had seen for the first time that morning. And it was a different voice that said, 'Hello, Paul.'

'Hello, Freda. Come in.'

'I'm . . . I'm sorry to hear that you have been ill.'

'Oh, it's nothing; just a touch of flu. Sit down, won't you?'

It was all so formal that Alison wanted to scream. She watched Paul indicate the chair that Mrs Gordon-Platt should take, and not until she was seated did he return to the couch. Then, looking over the back of it to where Alison was still standing, he said, 'You have met my ward already, so there's no need for any introductions.' He turned his face to the visitor now and added lightly, 'By the way, would you like coffee?'

'Yes. Yes, I would, thank you.'

Again he was looking over the back of the couch towards Alison. 'Tell Nellie, Alison, will you . . . as you go out? There's a good girl.'

She had to get out of the room at once. Good girl again! Treating her like a child, and dismissing her in that way!

As she stood in the little hall trying to compose

herself before going across to the kitchen to give Nellie Dickenson the order, the reason for her annoyance at being termed a girl came to her with devastating truth. She had for so long been mistress of this house that she considered she had ceased to be a girl many years ago. She had taken up the role of chatelaine with zest and metaphorically she had worn the keys at her belt; and one of those keys had locked her guardian and herself fast together. But now it looked as if she might have to hand that key over to someone else.

She turned her head at the sound of the voices coming from within the room. In the seconds she had been standing outside the door no-one had spoken. Had they just been sitting looking at each other? The woman's voice was so low that Alison only just caught the end of her words. 'And it's wonderful to see you again, Paul.'

Alison waited for the reply and when it came it eased the beating of her heart just the slightest. For Paul's voice was no longer smooth and easy; no longer was he the host receiving the unexpected guest. His voice was deep and harsh as he asked, 'Why have you come?'

The woman did not answer this question, but after a space she gave a little laugh and said, 'You haven't altered, Paul, not in all these years. You have so many faces. I always said the stage had lost an actor.'

'You haven't answered my question.'

The kitchen door opening caused Alison to scurry forward. As if Mrs Dickenson had surprised her at eavesdropping, she fumbled with her words as she said, 'Would you . . . Mr Paul . . . If you don't mind, Nellie, taking more coffee in, he has a visitor.'

'Oh, all right. But it means making fresh.' Mrs Dickenson turned her uncompromising body around and went back into the kitchen, as Alison, taking each stair slowly and thoughtfully, went down to the shop, there to meet Nelson eagerly awaiting her.

Nelson had a habit, when excited, of tapping his thumbnails together. This made a quaint sound, like the noise of a miniature woodpecker. And now to the tap-tap-tap he came forward, saying, 'Aa know who she is. She's changed. By lad, she's changed, but Aa recognised her. What does she want here?'

'You know as much as I, Nelson. But you say you knew her? When was that?'

'Oh, just afore the war. When she and Mr Paul . . .' He screwed up his small eyes at her. 'Perhaps this is news to you but that one' – he jerked his eyebrows upwards – 'and Mr Paul were thick enough at one time to be near married . . . Believe that? But what does she want now? Aa smell a rat. Aa was never much for her and Aa'm not likely to alter after twenty years. But, by! she's changed. Still good-looking though.' He jerked his head towards Alison. 'Aa wonder how he's taken it.'

He leant towards her again. 'What happened when she went in?'

'Nothing. Nothing much.'

'By lad, Aa wish Aa could have been there.'

'Nelson.' She took the old man's arm and led him away from the staircase door towards the centre of the shop as if she were escorting him to the street, but halfway down the drugget she drew him to a stop and asked quietly, 'How long did they know each other?'

'Nearly two years, Aa would say, but it was a high-powered two years from what Aa remember of it, for he was nuts about her. Aye' – Nelson shook his head slowly – 'there's no denying that. Clean stark staring-mad, he was. His old dad was worried, but he didn't live to see the end. Aa'd do anything for Mr Paul, give him me life. Aa would that – he knows Aa would – but in me heart Aa was glad at the time that things turned out as they did, 'cos there wouldn't have been any place for me here if he'd got her. Ooh!' The word was long drawn out. 'Aa knew that all right. Aa've knocked about a bit and Aa know people. You see Aa don't know whether you know this either, Miss Alison, but Aa was on the road; you know, a tramp. It was with the slump. All the shipyards were idle in the North, an' the mines an' all, and, with many a thousand other men, Aa tramped south. An' one winter night I came up the street here and you know where Farrow's, the wine shop, is now? Well, there was a café there then, and the smell knocked me clean out. Aye, it did.' Nelson laughed at the memory. 'Aa fell flat on me face and Aa woke up in the back shop here. Yes, in this very shop. Mr Paul's dad had carried me in and when Aa came round he gave me a feed. Aa offered to work to pay him for it and Aa asked him if he could give me a job. He said he was right sorry but he couldn't, as business was bad. This country was in an awful state then, miss. Paul at the time was still a lad at school. There was no Mrs Aylmer; she had died years ago. An' Aa saw that this place wanted cleaning up. Aa liked pieces of furniture. Me mother had had some nice pieces in the kitchen afore she had to sell them for bread and such, and Aa made old Mr Aylmer a proposition. Aa said to him "Give me one square meal a day and Aa'll work for you for nought." For after all, miss' – he brought his stooped shoulders further down and wagged his face in front of her as he gave voice to a profound truth – 'for after all, it's only heat and meat we live for, isn't it? Well, that's how Aa really started here, miss. And when Mr Paul had just turned sixteen his father died, an' he leaves school and takes over. Then comes the war, an' just havin' one eye they won't take me, so Aa do me stint as night watchman at Wheelers an' Aa look after the place here and buy a little bit when I can, so's to stock up for the time when he should come back and want to start again.'

Alison stopped the flow at this point and, patting him on the arm, she said softly, 'Yes, I know, Nelson. And Mr Paul appreciates all you've done. You can believe me he does.'

'Oh, Aa know that, miss. Aa know, for what he's done for me already. Aa'm set up for life now, with me two little rooms and me regular stint. Oh, as long as Mr Paul's alive Aa'll be all right. And he'll see me out, there's no doubt about that.'

'But what about the girl, Nelson? I mean, Mrs Gordon-Platt.' Alison probed, gently pushing the old man's memory backwards again.

'Oh, her. Well, Aa think that started when he was still at school, in the sixth form. You know, she was nothing. Her old man had a boot shop around Talbot Close, Carter they called him. But she was a looker and she had the lads after her. And Mr Paul was a looker too. They made a striking pair, as Aa remember. And then there was this fellow, Charles Platt . . . Gordon-Platt. He first came on Mr Paul's horizon on the football field, as far as Aa can gather. Mr Paul was captain of his school first eleven, and so was this bloke at his boarding school. And strange as it may seem, they struck up a friendship. Aa don't think Mr Paul knew who he was at first, and then he was a bit flattered like, and who wouldn't be, because afore the war the house where he lived was some place. Beacon Ride, just off the coast road.'

'Yes, yes, I know it, Nelson.'

'Well, it was a funny kind of friendship, for this other lad was nearly three years older than Mr Paul. Then just about the time Paul's dad died, this young fellow went up to Oxford. But he wasn't there long afore he got into mischief and was sent packing, and from then on he haunted this shop here and Mr Paul. Aa never knew the rights of it then. Mr Paul didn't talk to me in those days like he does now – we weren't close then – an' Aa hadn't had a chance to do very much for him. Besides, he was just a lad, and after all Aa was just a fellow his father had picked up in the street, and Aa couldn't expect to have much influence on him, nor for him to tell me anything that was troubling him. But as time went on Aa knew there was something afoot and it wasn't good. It was to do with the printing business. You know Burtons, the supermarket, in Pye Street?' Alison nodded. 'Well, that used to be a printing firm, and Aa had the surprise of me life when Aa found out that Mr Paul had bought it, him and this Charles Gordon-Platt. Aa didn't know the ins and outs but Aa know Aa was very puzzled at the time, and still am' – He nodded his head quickly at her – 'as to where the money came from, for to buy a printing business you need thousands and thousands, and this place' – he wagged his head about, indicating the shop – 'was bringing in hardly enough to pay the mortgage on it. An' then the balloon burst . . . When Mr Paul first got to know her' – the head was jerked upwards again – 'she was never out of this place. Hours an' hours an' hours she spent up those stairs with him. One time Aa thought Aa'd hint that they would get talked about, but Aa had enough sense to keep me mouth shut. And then this Charles fellow starts joining them. Mr Paul, he didn't seem to mind, for he was, in a sort of way, as daft about the Gordon-Platt bloke as he was about her. Then one day, it was just a couple of months afore war was declared, a man came to the shop and spent quite a long time upstairs with Mr Paul, and from that day nothing went right. After that, this man kept comin' and there was another bloke with him, a solicitor. At this time, Aa remember, she, Freda Carter as she was then, was on holiday at Dover, supposedly with an aunt, and Mr Charles Gordon-Platt was noticeably absent from the shop an' all. Well, the long and the short of it, Miss Alison, is that they never came back to the shop at all. They had run off together, an' believe it or not, it nearly knocked Mr Paul round the bend . . . See here.' He took her arm. 'Aa'll show you somethin'. You've seen them afore, but you'd never have guessed in a hundred years what they were caused by . . . Look at these here.' He had led her back down the shop to the door of the storeroom. The framework of the door was of heavy oak and passing through the top lintel was a beam that ran the whole width of the shop. The stanchion of the door and the beam were notched in several places as if by a chopper. 'See those?' Nelson pointed. 'Mr Paul did that. He had bought a lot of old stuff from a big house in Brighton. Aa helped him bring it in from the car. Old swords, a broken visor, stuff like that. It had been displayed in a private museum. He had pulled one of the swords from its scabbard when Aa remarked in a jocular way, like, "Mail from Dover there, Mr Paul." "Where?" He had the sword in his hand as Aa pointed. An' still with it in his hand he went over to the desk where Aa'd left the letter, an' laying down the sword he picked it up. Aa don't know from that day to this what was in that letter, but Aa do know its contents sent him stark-staring mad. Aa've seen men go barmy. Oh, aye, Aa have. Me uncle ended up in an asylum after upsetting a lamp over his wife, and her in bed with a newborn bairn. He went stark-staring mad and ran amok, and we searched the fells for him for two nights, but he had nothing on Mr Paul that day. For he took up that sword and he slashed at everything in sight. He ruined the only few decent pieces we had in the shop, and he finished up on that lintel. You know, Miss Alison' – Nelson bent towards her – 'if anybody had been in the shop that day, even if anybody had been passing by, they would have had him locked up. He went clean, stark-staring mad and then he turned on me, but Aa didn't bother to stay and argue. You couldn't see me for dust. Aa went out that back way and up the yard quicker than Aa'd moved in me life afore. Later Aa came round to the shop door, but it was locked. An' later again, Aa came back in case he had done himself an injury. Aa crept upstairs and there he was, sitting, just sitting, staring in front of him. An' you know something, Miss Alison, he looked as old that day as he does now. He has never grown any older. He jumped years that afternoon and he's stayed like that. Anyway, he has to me.'

'Oh, Nelson.' The tears were blinding Alison now, and she put her hand up and traced her fingers down the row of deep slashes in the lintel. 'To think he went through all that. I never guessed at any such thing.'

'No, you wouldn't. But Aa know Mr Paul. Aa know him better than anybody, even better than you, miss. He's a secret man, Mr Paul is. There are still things Aa can't fathom. Aa have always wondered what old Mr Tapley has on him.'

Alison swung round, rubbing at her eyes. 'You mean Bill Tapley's father?'

'Aye, miss. Bill Tapley's father. There was something funny there. Aa could never get to the bottom of it because Aa couldn't ask Mr Paul outright, not then Aa couldn't. Aa could now. Oh aye, Aa could now. But it's over and done with. Yet, at times, Aa still wonder what it was. Aa don't suppose you know, do you?' He cast his eyes sidewards at her.

'No, Nelson. No, I don't. And I'm just realising how little I know about Mr Paul. I really know nothing . . . Nothing.'

The old man leant towards her once more, and knocking his thumbnails together quickly he remarked, 'There's one thing Aa do know. Oh aye, Aa do know. He thinks the world of you; you've made a difference to his life. Aye, Aa do know that. He would be lost without you.'

Alison turned her back on the old man, saying to herself, 'I wonder, I wonder.'

'Ah, well.' Nelson sighed. 'There's goin' to be changes, Aa can feel it. Life becomes too pleasant, too easy, an' God says let's stir them up a bit, they've had it easy enough long enough. An' He sends somethin'. An' the somethin's arrived s'afternoon, if you ask me. Aye, well. We can do nought about it; Mr Paul'll go his own gait and take no notice of nobody, if I know him. An' Aa must go me road or else Aa'll never get that load back the day, will Aa? An' me yelling to be off ages ago . . . But you know something?' He was half-way down the shop again when he turned to her. 'Renault said Aa was getting too old to drive the van. What do you think of that?'

As Alison replied, 'That's nonsense, Nelson,' she thought, He may be right. But Nelson's age and his ability to drive the van were of little consequence to her at the moment. The only thing that mattered now was that the staircase door should open and Mrs Freda Gordon-Platt would emerge to leave the shop and not return. The horrible woman. As Paul had asked, Why had she come back? And to think that she had nearly driven him mad. He must ... he must have loved her with an intensity that wasn't quite normal. This thought deepened the ache in her chest and told her that here she had the reason for Paul not marrying. Vaguely she recalled rumours of women who had shown more than ordinary interest in him, but she had felt herself too secure in his affections to let them worry her. But Mrs Freda Gordon-Platt was no rumour. She was here in the flesh, attractively so. And would her power be any less today than it had been nearly twenty years ago? Oh, if only she would come. Why wasn't he throwing her out? ...

But Alison had some time to wait before Mrs Freda Gordon-Platt emerged. It was well over half an hour later when she heard the muffled footsteps on the stairs, and she was so worked up by this time that she could not allow herself to face Paul and the woman. So, moving swiftly, she went into the back shop.

They were talking when they entered the shop, quite amicably, like firmly established old friends. The sound of their level voices caused Alison's hand to press on her throat. She heard the footsteps pause and Mrs Gordon-Platt's voice say, 'Miss Read. I'd better say goodbye to her. Is she about?'

'No, I don't suppose so. She's likely gone out on one of her foraging expeditions. She's very keen.'

'Yes. Yes, she gave me that impression too . . . She's . . . she's an unusual looking girl, rather beautiful, in a miniature sort of way. She should be very attractive when she develops.'

Alison's fingers were pressing so tightly on her throat that she was forced to gulp. Then her lips formed into a tight line as Paul's voice came to her, his words in absolute accord with those of his visitor. 'Yes, I think you're right there. She should be quite something when she grows up.'

'Grows up!' Alison repeated the words to herself. Wait till she got him alone; just wait. She had been grown up for years and he knew it.

As the steps moved further away she crept towards the door, and standing to the side she could see the two figures outlined against the glass of the shop door. They were facing each other and Mrs Gordon-Platt was speaking. Alison couldn't quite catch all she was saying but the tail-end of her words came distinctly: 'As I said, youth is a crazy period, a period of false values and madness . . . blind madness. It's a pity that one is held accountable for the madness, though, isn't it? One suffers for being young . . . Age has it's compensations, don't you think so, Paul?'

'Yes, I do think so. Age, as you say, certainly has its compensations.'

Paul said something further, then Alison watched him take the outstretched hand and hold it. Then he opened the door and Mrs Freda Gordon-Platt turned and looked at him once again before leaving.

Alison now moved quietly forward and she watched Paul's eyes following the woman until she was out of view. When he turned to come down the shop she was waiting for him, and he stopped on the sight of her. For a moment he stood looking at her over the distance. It was an appraising look. Then he smiled before coming on, and when he was standing above her he bent forward and whispered, 'Well, did you get an earful?'

She had meant to go for him, saying, 'I'll be able to do a job of real work, I suppose, when I develop,' but she couldn't say a word for the simple reason that she saw on his face an expression she did not recognise. She had never seen this particular look before. It was a sort of . . . Inwardly, she turned away from the word, 'ecstatic'. Paul was happy. She could see it in his eyes, and the knowledge was like a scalpel probing her flesh. Paul was happy because he had taken up the threads of his old life . . . The girl who had nearly driven him mad had become a woman and had sought him out. The words came back to her. 'Youth is a period of false values,' she had said, and, 'Age has its compensations.'

Well, she wanted Paul to be happy, didn't she? She had always told herself that she would do anything in the world to further his happiness. There came to her the quaint, poignant words she had found embroidered on a piece of old silk. The cloth had been caught in the top of a bureau drawer, and she had been both intrigued and saddened as she read the story of a lost love. She had never forgotten the lines, and they seemed very appropriate to herself at this moment:

> His heart is a musical box.
> I lost the key;
> It was found by another.
> He bids 'Come joy with me.'

Come joy with me. Well, she was no Victorian heroine. She could not smile or be glib-tongued, feeling as she did. Yet she must not give herself away. If she did, their life together, or what was left of it, would be unbearable. So she fell into the role of chatelaine and nurse again, saying with harsh primness, 'If you catch another cold, don't expect me to go dizzy running round looking after you.' She watched him straining to keep the upturned corners of his mouth from rising further, but the laughter was deep in his eyes when he said, 'No, Matron, I won't expect you to go dizzy. I wouldn't for the world want you dizzy. I'm going back to the ward this instant.' He made a mock movement of scurrying away from her, but when he reached the staircase door he turned to her again and said, 'You remember what Dr Bailey prescribed two days ago? Champagne, he said. There is nothing like champagne for after-flu depression. You remember? And I told him I didn't need any champagne. But now, you know what?' He brought his brows down. 'You know, I think I do need that champagne. When Nelson comes back, slip across to Fuller's and buy a bottle.'

He did not wait for her reply but went swiftly through the door, and she stood with her hands tightly clasped before her, her teeth pulling in her lower lip, while a stern voice deep within her said, Now stop it! If you start crying at this stage where are you going to finish up? You might as well face it, you haven't seen the last of Mrs Freda Gordon-Platt. Look at it squarely and it will hurt less later on: she is here to stay.

Mrs Dickenson, as usual, had set the table and left everything for the evening meal. It was always something that could be quickly and easily done. Tonight it was grilled steak. These would take only a matter of minutes on the Aga grill pan. So when Alison refused

to stay and drink the proffered champagne, making
the excuse that she had to see to the steaks, Paul
said, 'What's your hurry? There's nothing spoiling.
Come on, drink up.' And he pressed the glass into her
hand, then picked up his own and lifted it towards
her, saying, 'I want you to drink to me. To the new
Paul Aylmer, who has this very day been rejuvenated.'
Bending down to her his voice now lost its bantering
tone and he said quietly, 'Drink up. I've got something
to tell you.' His eyes were looking deep into hers,
asking, she thought, for her understanding. Her heart
jolted against her ribs. She wanted to fly out of the
room. She just couldn't drink to what he was going
to tell her.

Reprieve came in the form of the distant sound of
the shop bell. It brought both their faces in the direction
of the hall. Paul's tone was one of irritation as he said,
'Who on earth can this be?'

'It could be anyone; it is only half-past seven.'
She was walking quickly out of the room as she
spoke. When she reached the bottom of the stairs
and switched on the shop light, she could see the
dark blur of a figure standing in the street. But it
wasn't until she actually opened the door that she
saw who it was, and then her eyes widened and her
mouth opened slightly in surprise.

He was wearing a pork-pie hat and a light overcoat
and looked younger than ever. He smiled disarmingly

at her and said somewhat shyly, 'I didn't find the treasure and I'm not jumping the stakes, so to speak. My visit is utterly legitimate.' When she did not answer, he shook his head slightly, adding, 'My mother asked me to call to see if she had left her compact. She remembers powdering her nose, after what I imagine was a little weep.' The look on his face was meant to encourage her to laugh with him at the foibles of their elders. 'I understand that my mother and Mr Aylmer had a happy and gruelling reunion raking up the past this afternoon.'

At this moment her mind was seething with suspicion. Left her compact? What an old trick! Yet, if the woman had worked this, she would herself have returned to retrieve the compact, wouldn't she? Why hadn't she? Why had she sent her son? Perhaps he had offered to come. He had likely seen it as an excuse to break the ice further; although they had met for only a few brief moments, she knew that this boy was interested in her; he had made it so plain. Unlike his mother, he appeared to be without guile. And anyway, she thought, she should be thankful to him, for he had stopped Paul, at least for the moment, from giving her the news that was apparently making him so happy.

'Don't look so disbelieving. My mother really has lost her compact. It happens to be a gold one and is of some value. If she didn't leave it here then she must have lost it on the bus, for she remembers sorting through her bag for the exact fare.'

'Come in.' Alison spoke flatly. Then after locking the door behind them she said, 'Will you come this way?'

When they reached the upper hall Paul was standing waiting at the door of the drawing-room, and he screwed up his eyes at the sight of the young man.

'This is Mr Gordon-Platt, Paul.'

'Oh?' Paul's eyes ranged over the young man, and in turn he himself was scrutinised.

'Good evening, sir. I've heard quite a lot about you from my mother.' The hand was extended deferentially.

'How do you do? Come in.' After a handshake Paul turned about and the young man followed. Alison, bringing up the rear, said, 'Mrs Gordon-Platt thinks she left her compact here this afternoon. Have you seen it?'

'Her compact?' Paul turned and looked from Alison to the young man, then back to Alison again and said, 'No, I haven't seen any compact.'

'Where was she sitting?' Alison had the feeling she was presiding over an investigation.

'In that chair there.' He pointed to the big armchair to the side of the fireplace, then walked towards it and, looking down, said, 'There's nothing here.' Bending forward now he picked up the cushion and shook it. 'She can't have left it . . . But wait a minute. Look.' He pointed, and there, trapped between the framework and the upholstery, was a circular gold object. Picking it up, he held it in his hand for a moment and looked at it thoughtfully before handing it to the young man, saying, 'I wonder how that happened. I didn't notice her upset her bag.'

'Oh, she's always laying things down and forgetting about them. She's very absent-minded in that way.'

Absent-minded. Mrs Gordon-Platt absent-minded? Alison couldn't imagine it. And yet there would have been no point in leaving her compact unless she were going to return for it herself. She felt that she was being unjust to the woman, on this point at any rate. And to make amends, and also because she didn't want to be alone with Paul, she decided to extend an invitation. Anything rather than have to listen to what Paul had to tell her. So she said, 'We were just about to eat. Would you care to join us?'

'Really . . . I would love it. But will you have . . . ? Well, what I mean—'

'Oh, we have enough. I will cut down on Paul's share. He eats far too much anyway.' As she spoke she did not look at Paul but walked out of the room. In the kitchen she put the hot soup into a tureen and the steaks on the grill pan, added another plate and bowl to the hot rack, then stood watching the steam hissing fiercely from the pan. And she likened the fierce heat that was sealing in the juices of the steaks to the anguish that was sealing off her natural spontaneity. This morning, when she had woken up, life had been good, wonderful, the day ahead much too short. Now, looking back on it, it had been long and filled with surprising and frightening crevices of pain. And today was but a beginning, for if Paul again took up with Mrs Gordon-Platt . . . If he married her, and taking up with her once more could only lead to that, then what would there be to live for? Some wise sage would tell her she was young, that she would forget, she would marry and have a family. The only family she wanted was Paul. The only man she wanted to marry was Paul . . . There, it was out, she had said it to herself. Her thoughts and feelings over the years had flown round this truth like a moth round a flame, advancing and retreating, advancing and retreating. And now the moth had gone into the centre of the flame and been burnt up. *She* was being burnt up. There'd be nothing left of her when she lost Paul, for she would have no family, no-one in the world belonging to her. She knew that this latter thought possessed a thick coating of self-pity, but if she didn't pity herself who would pity her? She had no-one to turn to, no relatives in whom she could confide. As her thinking reached this point she had a mental picture of the elder Mrs Gordon-Platt and the old maid, together with the faded velvet high-backed chair, and she blinked her eyes as she wondered why she should think that this combination should present itself as a symbol of a family. For a moment her mind darted from her own worry and tried, as it had done earlier in the day, to catch at some thread that would tell her where, before, she had seen the two old women and the chair.

The time clock rang, warning her that the steaks were ready. Within a few minutes she was carrying the tray through the door which led into the dining section of the long room, and glancing along its length she saw that Paul was sitting listening to Mr Gordon-Platt, who was saying, 'No, not in England. I was born in Mexico, of all places. My father went there straight from here. We lived there until I was ten; the business went flat. My father wasn't a very good businessman, I'm afraid. It's been my mother who has had to do all the thinking, all the time.' There came a little laugh here. 'She might be absent-minded and leave things about, but she's got a very good head for business. If she'd had half a chance she would have pulled us through. But there it is. I'm glad to be in England, anyway.'

'You had never been in England before you came to Beacon Ride?' Paul was asking the question with stiff politeness.

'Oh, yes. I first came to England when I was fifteen.

I was at school here for three years and then I went back to Italy.'

'It must have been expensive keeping you at school in England.' There was more than a touch of cool politeness in Paul's voice now.

'Yes, I suppose so. But my mother was wonderful. She squeezed the coffers dry to give me a start.'

'A start? To what? What are you going to do?'

'Well, I really wanted to take up art, but that is out of the question now. Unless you're a natural-born Picasso you can't get into that line without having enough money to keep you going until you strike it lucky. When my grandfather's will brought us back here, I thought ... well, that was that, everything was cut and dried for me. Of course, I hadn't seen the place then.'

Into the uneasy silence Alison said, 'Come along and get it while it's hot.'

It couldn't be said that the supper was a gay affair, or even a passably pleasant meal, but it certainly wasn't the fault of Roy Gordon-Platt, for in his diffident way it was really he who kept the conversation going, asking questions of Paul with suitable deference, mostly questions concerning the business. He confessed to being ignorant with regard to antiques, admitting that his knowledge went back only as far as the early-Victorian period.

Alison had expected Paul to explain that early

Victorian furniture now came under the heading of antiques, but Paul, she noticed with uneasiness, had fallen into one of his stiff silences. Perhaps it was because of Roy's manner, for he called him 'sir' all the time. Although this was perhaps good manners, it was also openly giving deference to an older man, a man old enough to be his father, a man who might have been his father. Did Roy know this? Whether he did or not there was one thing she was vitally aware of: Paul did not like the boy, whereas the more she herself saw of him, the more she took to him.

The meal over, she made no attempt to clear away, for what conversation there was was now solely between herself and Roy, and she did not want to leave him to the mercy of Paul's stark silence. As much as she loved Paul, at times in the past she'd had her work cut out to endure these herself.

It was about half-past nine when Roy took his departure. As he shook hands with Paul he said, 'I hope we'll meet again soon, sir.'

To this Paul merely inclined his head; then after a moment, he said, 'Goodbye.'

Alison led the way down the stairs through the shop to the door, and after she had opened it, Roy, holding her hand in farewell, asked, 'Do you like music?'

'It all depends what kind it is.' She was smiling at him.

'There's a symphony concert on at the Burley Hall

for the next three evenings, starting tomorrow. I was thinking of going. Would you care to come?' His face took on a solemn look as he added, 'You'd be doing me a favour, for I feel rather at a loose end at times, and that's putting it mildly. Believe me, I get frantic sitting in that mausoleum, especially in the evenings.'

She could understand this and she felt in sympathy with him. Yet if he had given her this invitation two nights ago she would have refused it point-blank. But since his mother had complicated her life, and since Paul, to use his own words, had become rejuvenated by her appearance, she almost grabbed at the invitation. 'I'd love to,' she said. 'I haven't been to a concert for months. In fact, I haven't been out anywhere for months ... Yes, I would love to.' As she said this, Alison knew she was setting the seal on the already changed way of life in this house.

'Oh, good. Good.' The look on his boyish face, expressing his evident pleasure and enthusiasm, was very flattering, but a little embarrassing.

She said quickly, 'Goodbye. It's been pleasant having you here this evening.'

His face became solemn and he spoke almost under his breath as he said, 'You're a very kind person, aren't you?'

'We won't go into the traits of my character at this time of night.' She laughed to cover her embarrassment. 'Goodbye. Oh! Will you call here for me? And when is it? Are you going tomorrow?'

'Yes. Yes, of course. Tomorrow night. I'll call about seven. All right?'

'All right.' She watched him for a moment as he moved reluctantly away, and because she knew he was going to turn to see if she was still standing there, she stepped back into the shop and swiftly closed the door. At the staircase door she put out the shop light and stood in the darkness for a moment, bracing herself, as it were, before she faced Paul again. She knew he was annoyed and his mercurial change of manner always affected her.

Slowly she climbed the stairs and went into the room. He seemed to be waiting for her. His silent mood must have passed for he greeted her stonily with, 'Well, have you enjoyed yourself?'

She reared against the aggressive tone and also the unfairness of his attack. He could be merry and bright after a visit from Mrs Gordon-Platt, but she apparently wasn't to enjoy the son's company. Why? His whole attitude, to say the least, was strange. If he was interested in Freda Gordon-Platt then it was going to be awkward for him if he didn't like her son. She gave him no direct answer to his question but burst out, 'What do you want, anyway? You can't have everything your own way.'

'What do you mean?' He brought his brows down at her.

'Just what I say ... Talking me down with ... with others, just as if I were an infant, or a gauche girl, fresh from school ... All right!' She bounced her head at him. 'If you consider me so young ... quite *undeveloped*' – she stressed the word – 'then it is better that I associate with others of my age, don't you think? ... Yes, I enjoyed myself tonight, and for your information, I like him. I think you would at least know where you stood with him.'

Before her mouth had snapped shut, she was sorry for what she had said. Although she saw that Paul was still angry, his expression showed plainly that she had hurt him, and deeply. Impulsively she was about to move forward, her hand outstretched in contrition, when he turned from her and walked down the room and out through the dining-room door. Clearly, he had gone this way to avoid passing her. A few seconds later she heard his bedroom door close with a bang.

Oh dear! dear! dear! She covered her face with her hands. Why was everything going wrong?

She was walking slowly towards the fire when the phone rang. It was in the hall, and when she lifted the receiver and heard a voice speaking her name, her eyes widened. The voice was saying, 'Is she in ... Miss Read?'

'Miss Read speaking.'

'Oh . . . oh. This is Miss Beck, Miss Read. You remember me?'

'Oh yes, Miss Beck, I remember you. Of course.'

There was silence on the line now and Alison said, 'Hello, are you there?'

'Yes. Yes, I'm here, Miss Read. I . . . I wonder if you could manage to come and see me.'

Alison withdrew the mouthpiece slightly away from her face, puzzled by the request, then said, 'Yes. Yes, of course, Miss Beck. When would you like me to come? I could pop over tomorrow afternoon.'

'No, no, that wouldn't do. You see . . . Well, it's like this. I want you to come when Mrs Charles is out. I'm phoning now because I have the house to myself. You understand?'

Alison nodded, and then said quickly, 'Yes. Yes, of course, Miss Beck.'

'It's important that I see you, and soon. Something . . . something awful has happened.'

'Awful?' Alison had a picture of the old lady lying on the drawing-room floor and covered with blood. She said quickly, 'Is Mrs Gordon-Platt worse?'

'No. No, she's all right now, but if she finds out I'm meeting you it'll kill her. Could you come tomorrow evening at about seven? Mrs Charles will be out then; I heard her making an appointment. And Mr Roy goes out most evenings.'

Tomorrow evening? Mr Roy would indeed be out

tomorrow evening and she would be with him. She said, 'I'm afraid I couldn't manage tomorrow evening, Miss Beck, I've an appointment then. I'm sorry.'

'Oh dear.' The anxiety in the voice was plain, and then Miss Beck said hurriedly, 'I go to the post office in Crossly Down for my pension tomorrow morning. I'll be there about ten o'clock. Do you think you could meet me then?'

As Alison said quickly, 'Yes. Yes, I could manage that, Miss Beck,' she thought how odd it was that a woman living in that mansion – although it was falling to bits it was still a mansion – had to go to the post office for her pension. It didn't fit in somehow.

Miss Beck was speaking again. 'Perhaps you could take me a little way in your car and then I could tell you.'

'Yes. Yes, I'll do that, Miss Beck.'

The voice on the phone had been whispering most of the time and Alison found herself following suit.

As Miss Beck spoke again, saying earnestly, 'You won't forget, Miss Read, will you?' Alison heard Paul's door open, and she said quickly, 'No. No, of course not, I'll be there.'

The voice came again, saying hesitantly now, 'May I ask you not to tell Mr Aylmer? You see, he might . . . well, he might tell Mrs Charles and I wouldn't want that. You'll understand when I've told you all about it.'

'Yes, yes, I understand.' Paul was standing at the far side of the landing now and Alison said quickly, 'Good night. Good night, I'll be there.'

As Alison put the phone down, Paul asked briefly, and in a much modified tone, 'Business?'

'No. No.' She turned from the telephone table. 'It was for me.'

'Oh.' The stiffness was back in the voice again. '*He* didn't lose much time. He couldn't have got home yet. He must have used a call-box.' He dropped his head forward slightly now and his eyes narrowed at her. 'You said you'd be there. Are you seeing him again?'

Alison swallowed to give herself time. 'Yes. Yes, he asked me to go to a concert at Burley Hall tomorrow evening.'

They stood facing each other; then in a surprisingly calm and unemotional voice Paul said, 'Very nice for you. I hope you enjoy it.' At this he turned away and went down the stairs again, and Alison repeated to herself: What does he want? He can't have it both ways. Was he, she asked herself, seeing himself married to Mrs Gordon-Platt with herself living on here as a step-daughter? The very idea was nauseating, and it angered her. She now marched into the drawing-room, put the screen up before the fire, turned the lights out and then went downstairs to her own room.

A little while later, when she was settled comfortably in bed, she found she could not sleep. She was conscious of Paul in his room across the landing, for she guessed that he too was awake and lying thinking . . . But thinking of what?

It was around one o'clock in the morning when she turned her face into the pillow and murmured, 'Oh, Paul! Oh, Paul!' All annoyance and temper had left her. All she wanted was to wake up in the morning and find him standing beside her bed saying, as he usually did, 'Come on, wake up! you lazy little monkey, you. Come on now, don't let that tea get cold,' and to hear herself softly snuffling and snorting in reply. Then to drink her tea in utter contentment and hear him pottering about in the kitchen above her head. But that would never happen again, never. She kept repeating, 'Oh, Paul! Oh, Paul!' until at last she fell asleep.

Three

THE CAR WAS PARKED ON THE GRASS VERGE ON the outskirts of the village, giving Alison a view of the cluster of houses and the post office. She leaned back in her seat and waited. She wished she smoked. Perhaps she would try again some time. The heating was off now and her knees were cold; she wished she had brought a rug. She looked in the pocket of the door: there wasn't a magazine or paper in it. She had cleared them all out when she had cleaned the car the other day. She wished she had brought something to read. Oh, wishing, wishing, wishing. She shook her head at herself. 'If wishes were diamonds I'd make you a crown, and build you a carriage and take you to town.' The jingle from her childhood came back to her. She remembered playing hop-scotch to it in the yard of her uncle's shop and her uncle patting her head and saying, 'Never give up wishing; if you want a thing hard enough, you'll get it. Go on wishing and you'll build your crown' . . . She didn't want a crown. What was the use of a crown? All she wanted was that time would go back three days, even two, and then things would be the same again between Paul and herself.

As the wind whistled past the car windows she thought solicitously, 'Oh, I wish he wasn't going out; it's too early; this wind will cut through him.' He had surprised her at breakfast by saying, 'I'm off to Eastbourne this morning.'

It had been his habit over the years to visit Eastbourne at least once a week, even when there wasn't an auction taking place. He called it his scrounging day. She had never been asked to accompany him on these trips. When she was a child she had never questioned his going off on his own, and when she grew up she had looked upon it as one of the foibles of a man. He usually took his scrounging day on a Wednesday and today was a Wednesday.

At this point in her thinking, she suddenly saw the shabbily dressed, stooped figure of Miss Beck coming along the road towards her, so she hastily stepped out of the car and waited for her approach. The woman looked even older, if that was possible. She also looked cold and tired. Alison's pity mounted; the poor soul wanted someone to look after her; instead, she was taking care of that selfish old woman. And she did think that Mrs Gordon-Platt was a selfish old woman.

As she settled Miss Beck in the passenger seat of the car she said apologetically, 'I'm sorry I don't have a rug to wrap around your legs.'

'Oh, that's all right. It's quite all right. I'm not cold,' replied Miss Beck.

'Well, now.' Alison turned to her from her seat. 'Here we are. How can I help you?'

Miss Beck looked at her grey gloved hands for a moment before she began picking nervously at a thumb. Then jerking her body squarely round to Alison, she began hurriedly, 'Mrs Charles . . . she's taken some of madam's things . . . to sell . . . Oh, I don't really blame her. She's in an awful state, really. I could feel sorry for her in a way. No, I don't really blame her, but she's taken the tea-caddy.'

'The tea-caddy?' Alison moved her head in enquiry.

'Yes. It doesn't look anything, but it's old, more than a hundred years, perhaps two, I don't really know. But it isn't just the tea-caddy itself; it happens to be where madam hid half of the collar when she broke it up.'

Alison's mouth drooped just the slightest in her

bewilderment, then she repeated, 'The collar? What kind of a collar?'

'It wasn't really a collar; madam just called it that. It was a necklace. She kept it hidden so that she would have something left, something to fall back on. She broke it in two and divided it between the tea-caddy and the writing-case. It was when she knew Mrs Charles was coming. You see, it was the only thing of real value madam had left and she wanted it for Miss Margaret.'

'Miss Margaret?' said Alison, in further bewilderment.

'Yes, that's madam's daughter. She only had the one son and one daughter. Madam was keeping the necklace for her. She daren't put it in the bank; the bank swallows up everything.' Miss Beck shook her head mournfully at this, then went on, 'We took the brass top off the writing-case. It was heavily embossed and so the stones fitted quite well underneath. We wrapped them in cotton wool and twisted the setting ... they were narrow, gold-linked chains; we twisted them this way and that like a jigsaw puzzle. It was very interesting and it took us nearly two days to get them fitted in. And then the other half we left as it was and put in the tea-caddy. There's a panel in the lid. I never knew of it until madam showed me. It's very ingenious. No-one would ever guess, as the whole thing looks too thin. And you work the springs by pressure on the glass containers. It's very ingenious, very.'

'And Mrs Charles has taken the tea-caddy?' Alison asked quietly.

'Yes, with two Sèvres plates and five Doultonware. It doesn't matter about those; it's the tea-caddy that's important. You see, madam had her own sitting-room upstairs. She had lots of nice pieces in there, but she had to sell quite a number herself, and then yesterday I noticed immediately that the tea-caddy had gone. You see, I always look at the tea-caddy, knowing what it holds. I nearly went distracted . . . distracted. And I daren't tell madam, and I don't know what I'll do if she asks for it. It would kill her, I know it would kill her if she lost them too . . . the stones. You see, she lost the other half that's in the writing-case. It was when she was in hospital. We all thought she was dying, which is why Mrs Charles cleared her room. I would have tried to stop Mrs Charles but I was at the hospital with madam, and when I came back the two cabinets had gone, and other things too. The cabinets used to stand at each side of madam's bed and they were filled with . . .' Miss Beck stopped her rambling at this point and shook her head slowly as she smiled a little pathetically. Then, nodding at Alison, she said, 'Those cabinets were filled with memories, memories going back over sixty years, since madam was seventeen or so. I became part of those memories when I was fourteen. I started in the kitchen at Beacon Ride the same year madam came there as a bride, and she took a fancy to me and trained me to be her maid. I've travelled the world with her.' Again Miss Beck shook her head. 'It was a wonderful life until Mr Charles came down from Oxford. And then the war came. Nothing has been the same since.'

Miss Beck, Alison saw, was about to go further and further back into the past and she wanted to keep her in the present. Quietly she prompted, 'Have you said anything to Mrs Charles about her taking the things, Miss Beck?'

'Yes. Yes, I have. I told her she must bring them back. But of course I didn't tell her about the tea-caddy.'

'What did she say?'

'She said she was selling them and that she had already taken them to the auction rooms; but she wouldn't tell me where. What she did say was that I must get something out of madam or she would have to sell more things. And I told her, as I've told her before, that madam hasn't any money. She's in a great deal of debt. The small income that she's living on hardly pays for the food. I myself pay Mrs Connor. She comes in in the morning to do the cooking and odd jobs, you know.'

'Who pays *you*, Miss Beck?' Alison was smiling gently and now Miss Beck returned the smile. It wavered pathetically around her wrinkled face as she answered, 'I've forgotten; it's so long since I was paid, in money that is, but I've been paid a thousandfold in other ways. As long as I have madam that's all the payment I want.'

What loyalty. Alison's throat became tight as she looked at Miss Beck. A lifetime given up in gratitude for the doubtful pleasure of being a lady's maid. This kind of loyalty was rare and would undoubtedly die with the generation to which it belonged. Putting her hand out, she patted the grey gloves, saying, 'You want me to find out where Mrs Charles has sold or is selling these things, and get them back for you?'

'Yes. Yes, please. Oh, please. I don't know how much you'll have to pay, but well . . . well, I can give you the money. You see, I have a little nest-egg put by.' Her face was solemn. 'It's not much, but I've always felt there might come a time when madam would need it. I have thirty-five pounds. I don't suppose the china and the caddy will sell for anything near that, but I just want you to know that I can pay you. You see, Mrs Charles must have the money that the objects fetch.'

Thirty-five pounds . . . a nest egg in this age! 'Don't worry.' Alison slowly patted the glove again. 'There are only four plates, you say?'

'No, five. And one is like a fruit dish. And, of course, the caddy.'

'Well, depending on their condition I should say they'd fetch anything between five and ten pounds.

That is if they are being sold at auction. Do you think she may have sold them privately?'

'I don't think so. She would hate the idea of going to a shop to sell something; she thinks it's different putting them into a sale.'

'Have you any idea where she took them?'

'Not really. She was in Eastbourne yesterday, and Brighton the day before.'

'Well, if she put them up for auction they'll be out in the catalogues shortly. There'll be plenty of time to go round and have a look. Also, I'll make enquiries at the showrooms and if they haven't been catalogued yet I may be able to buy them back straight away.'

'Oh, thank you, thank you. You are very good. If it could only be soon. For I don't think madam could stand up to the shock. You see, the stones are, in a way, her conscience.'

'Her conscience?'

'Yes. She's always had Miss Margaret on her conscience, not Mr Charles. She spoilt Mr Charles, and look what he did. But she never spoilt Miss Margaret. She was never nice to Miss Margaret. I was always sorry for Miss Margaret. I did what I could, but my loyalty lay with madam. You can understand that?'

Alison nodded and asked, 'What happened to . . . to Miss Margaret?'

'Well, she was twenty-three when the war broke out. And she upset madam right away by becoming a Land Girl. She worked on the farms round about here and stayed at home. I thought she was fortunate in that way, but perhaps I was mistaken. She was a plain-looking girl, was Miss Margaret – not like madam. Madam was beautiful when she was young – and she was quiet, withdrawn; madam didn't understand her. After the war she tried to do things round the estate, but it was like one beaver trying to dam the Nile. At one time there had been three gardeners up at the house, not to mention the boys in training. The head gardener was a man named Welsh. His little house was just down the lane there.' She pointed. 'He had a son called Robert. After the war, Robert went to work on a farm . . . that one just over the way there.' She pointed again. 'The land adjoins that of the estate, at least what was our boundary in those days. Well, this Robert and Miss Margaret came across each other at times. In fact, the times spread into five years and then one day Miss Margaret came to her mother and said she wanted to marry Robert Welsh and madam's reply was to show her the door. You see, this was the second time that such a thing had happened to madam, for there was Mr Charles too. He had married very much benea . . . what I mean to say is, he was a disappointment. Well, Miss Margaret married Mr Welsh. They didn't live in the cottage, but went away. There were a number of letters from Miss Margaret, but madam didn't answer them. It was not until madam knew that Mr Charles had died without making any effort to write or come and see her that she came to realise just how very good Miss Margaret had been to her in the past. She has a strong sense of justice, has madam, no matter how she may appear to other people. It was then she decided that Margaret must have the necklace, but she couldn't find her. I did put a notice in the paper, but it brought no result. And as you know madam hasn't the money for an investigator. The day when we split up the necklace madam said to me, "If we don't hear of her whereabouts before I go, Beck, you must keep the tea-caddy and the writing case. You can say I gave them to you. But you must keep them until she returns, for she'll come home one day. She'll leave that individual one day and come home, you'll see . . . you'll see." I remember Miss Margaret when she was about six . . .'

Miss Beck had forgotten she was sitting in a car talking to a complete stranger. She was now well settled in the past and she went on and on rambling about the virtues of Miss Margaret, while Alison thought again, Poor Miss Beck. That was to be her reward for a lifetime of service. To keep a few jewels for the daughter who had run away with a man. And it was that daughter's place, Alison thought harshly, to be looking after her mother, not this poor old thing. Her own troubles seemed slight now, and her life exciting compared with that of Miss Beck's. She said gently, 'I'll run you to the gates.'

'Oh, no, no. Oh, please, no.' Miss Beck came hastily out of the past. 'I really shouldn't have stayed so long here, but there's no-one about. I wouldn't want anyone to see us together, especially Mrs Charles . . . you know what I mean? And should you find the tea-caddy, or where it is, please don't phone me. Some time when I know I have the house to myself, I'll phone you. Will that be in order?'

'Yes; yes, of course.'

Alison now helped Miss Beck from the car and after assuring her once more that she would do all in her power to recover the tea-caddy, she stood watching the bent old figure scurrying along the road.

When she was once more in the car she sat thinking for a moment. She had the day before her; Nelson could manage all right, and Paul would be in Eastbourne until this evening. What was to prevent her from having a look round straight away? She could keep her eyes open for other things at the same time. She would go to Brighton first. It was no use picking up catalogues. It was much too early for the items to have been listed, but she knew the auctioneers in at least two of the salerooms and she would ask them about them. If she couldn't see the auctioneers themselves the porters would be helpful. Then there were two auction rooms in Eastbourne that she knew of, as well as one in Bexhill and two in Hastings. She would make the rounds.

At half-past four in the afternoon Alison came to the end of her round in the Claremont Auction Rooms in Hastings. She found the porters in the midst of what she recognised to be a new intake of items. To the untrained eye it looked as if they would never get the jumble straightened into neat rows around the walls and an orderly formation down the centre of the room. One of the porters was known to her and she said, 'Hello, Fred. I wonder if you could help me?'

'Will if I can, miss,' he replied laconically, a manner which seemed to be prevalent amongst porters. Then when she told him what she was looking for, he answered, 'Well, not so far as I've seen, miss. No Sèvres pieces in this time, not down here, anyway; but there's no knowing what's upstairs. Mr Luckin's up there cataloguing now. Why not try him?'

She thanked him and made her way upstairs. This room was kept solely for antiques. And it was Paul who came once a month to do the buying here. Mr Luckin, the assistant auctioneer, was a young man with an attractive smile and a sense of humour. She had spoken to him on one or two occasions before. He said now, 'Hello, miss. Come for a preview?'

When she told him what she had come about he shook his head slowly. 'Tea-caddy? Sèvres plates?

Doulton? No. Not a thing like that this time. Sèvres stands out like a sore thumb these days. It's getting noticeably rarer. You know, I have dreams at night, and they are all concerned with catalogues, and in one dream in particular I have reached lot 840 and every piece has been Sèvres.'

She laughed with him. It was a happy laugh. When their laughter had subsided he asked seriously, 'Someone put you on to it?'

'Well, not exactly. I'm not wanting it for the shop, it's –' she paused, how would she put it? 'It's a family affair and you know what family affairs are.' She herself didn't, but who was to know that? 'What's yours is mine. Well, one of them has put some pieces into a sale and another member of the family wants them back.'

'Oh. Any harm in asking the family name?'

She looked at him for a moment. Auctioneers, she had found, were in some cases the equivalent of doctors and priests. They could keep their tongues still when necessary. She said briefly, 'The Gordon-Platts from Beacon Ride.'

'Oh, Lordy!' She watched him as he beat his forehead with the palm of his hand. 'Some more of that . . . The younger one?'

'You know the younger Mrs Gordon-Platt?'

'I should say. Had a bit of trouble here a short while back through her. She put in a pair of Sheraton mahogany card tables.'

'I know; we bought them. I've got them in our drawing-room now. They are a lovely set.'

'You've got them? Well, well. But you didn't get the bedside cabinets, did you?' She shook her head.

'Well, it was those that caused the trouble. They were a nice pair, lovely. They weren't bought by the trade – someone private got them – but they were no sooner gone than a solicitor arrived. He was acting for the old lady. Apparently the young one thought the old one was going to snuff it and prematurely started selling up. But it wasn't the cabinets they wanted back as much as the contents. Anyway, we traced the buyer, who lived in Rye. But he had bought the cabinets legally, and naturally he didn't want to part with them. And this the solicitor didn't mind at all. It was what had been in the cabinets that he was interested in. But, believe it or not, the Rye man had sold the contents to somebody in this very room before he moved the cabinets. You know how it is when you've made a good buy and there's some rubbish attached, you pass it on, and this is what happened to the stuff inside the cabinets. Anyway, who would put any value on a batch of old snapshot albums, forty-seven of them to be correct? We've never traced them since, because the man who bought them, well, he—'

'You said albums? Snapshot albums?' Alison put in quietly.

'Yes. They did some hoarding in those days, didn't they? I didn't see them myself, but one of the porters said they were just ordinary snaps of holidays, hundreds and hundreds of them, all stuck in these albums. Apparently the bloke who bought them was also a private buyer, although he wasn't a regular and none of us could remember what he looked like; nor could the man in Rye, and he didn't even know his name, never thought about asking it . . . Well, he wouldn't, would he? So there it is . . . You cold?'

Alison had shivered, and she answered quickly 'No. No. Somebody walking over my grave, I think.' They laughed again. And now Mr Luckin said gravely, 'That madam's going to get herself into a packet of trouble if she doesn't wait for the old girl to die before she starts selling her up. A bit cold-blooded, don't you think?'

'I imagine they're very short of money.'

'Well, aren't we all? But we don't go round selling our mother's bits and pieces before she's cold. Anyway, I hope you come across them. But who'll be paying for them?'

'The personal maid, Miss Beck. She's very attached to her mistress. She doesn't want her to find out that the things are missing.'

'Kind hearts are better than coronets.' Once more they laughed, and Alison said, 'Well, thank you very much, Mr Luckin. It looks pretty hopeless, but I'll keep on.'

'I wish you luck. Goodbye.'

'Goodbye, and thanks again.'

When Alison got down the stairs and into the street she was still shivering, but not because someone was continuing to walk over her grave. She was shivering with excitement. The snap albums, forty-seven of them. Now she knew; now she knew where she had seen Mrs Gordon-Platt before, *and* Miss Beck, *and* the high-backed chair. She took to her heels and ran along the street to where the car was parked. All those albums and the embossed writing-case were at this moment in the storeroom of the shop. She had bought them herself in a job lot in the basement of the saleroom at Sealock. It was in the basement where all the junk was sold, where you could get anything from three to ten articles going in one lot, and where one of the articles might be a tea-chest full of albums. She had really gone for the lot because among them were three old English china cups in perfect condition. There were also seven glass decanters without stoppers, fourteen chipped dinner plates, a box of books and . . . a tea-chest full of snap albums. How the tea-chest had come to be in amongst all the other articles, she didn't know. She could only guess that the buyer in the first place had thought he was on to something – it wasn't unusual to make finds in the cupboards, or drawers of old furniture. Likely he was a dealer in a small way. But she now asked herself, as she sped along the main road towards home: if the man had been a dealer, would he have returned the albums to a sale, together with the old china cups? No dealer would have put those cups in the sale. No, it was more than likely he had been a private buyer . . . But why try to puzzle it out? She had got the albums, she had got Mrs Gordon-Platt's embossed writing-case. It seemed almost too good to be true . . .

When she dashed into the shop Nelson looked up from a paper he was reading, peered with his one eye over the top of his glasses and exclaimed, 'By! when you do come back we know you're here. What's your hurry?'

'That tea-chest with the albums, Nelson. You haven't touched it?'

'Well, as a matter of fact Aa—'

'Oh! Nelson. Don't . . . don't tell me you've sold them?'

'Sold them! No, of course not. Who'd want to buy them? We'd have to put a sixpenny tray out to sell them. Aa thought of dumping them.'

Alison let out a deep breath of relief and now walked slowly into the back shop. Crossing to a dark corner, she spotted the chest. There were the albums, some on their sides, some end up, all higgledy-piggledy. Quickly she began lifting them out and stacking them. And then she came to the brass-fronted writing-case. Supporting it in one hand, she gently traced her fingers over the design. It was the Prince of Wales's feathers; they filled each corner, and in the middle was a crown all stamped out on the brass. The case itself was worthless except as an ornament on a desk. It was cumbersome and she doubted if it had ever been used for the purpose it was made, but under these feathers, under this crown, lay part of a necklace. It was fantastic. This was a dealer's story. This was a dealer's tall-tale. This was the kind of find that buyers talked about in the recess between long sales as they snatched a meal before returning to dig in the gold pit of the auction room . . . 'Did you hear what happened to so-and-so?' would begin the fairy tale. 'He bought a picture; seventeen and six, he paid for it, and not a penny more. It was an original Corot . . . Fact!'

The tea-chest had been lot number three. The early lots, like the later ones, generally went cheap. The auctioneer usually threw them off quickly as a draw, for towards the end, cheap lots often meant boredom, cold feet, tiredness or hunger. But on that particular day she had had to pay £2.15s for number three, which she didn't consider cheap at all, and all because of the three old English cups. Paul had thought it a poor buy because, he said, they wouldn't make more than 30 shillings on the cups, as they were without saucers. Yet her £2.15s had bought a small fortune.

Nelson, coming to the doorway, said, 'You're lucky you know, Aa nearly dumped them, Miss Alison, Aa nearly did.'

She said to him, 'Here, stack the albums on my arms.'

'Afore you take your clothes off?'

'Afore Aa take me clothes off,' she mimicked. 'Come on, stack them up.'

She had to make three journeys down to the shop before all the albums were in the drawing-room, and when she had dumped the last pile on the hearthrug, Mrs Dickenson, surveying them, said, 'What on earth do you want to bring that junk up here for? I thought you were against messing the place up.'

'I want to look at the photos.'

'All them snaps? It would take you a year.'

'No, it won't; I'll be through them this evening; I'll have them out of your way by tomorrow. Don't worry.'

'I'm not worried, but if you leave them there, I'm not moving them when I dust.' As the door closed on Mrs Dickenson Alison smiled, and, settling herself on the floor, she picked up the brass-backed writing case and with a sense of awe she again traced her fingers over it. She would not attempt to open it until Paul came in. He was expert at finding notches or springs, or prising off delicate panels without leaving a mark. There was not the slightest doubt in her mind as to what lay beneath this embossed brass cover. She laid the case almost reverently down beside her, then began sorting the albums. She spread them around her, on the couch, the chairs, the hearthrug, all forty-seven of them. Some of the albums were large, being over a foot wide, others were only a few inches in length. But all were similar in that they had a date pasted on the back.

After some time, and a lot of juggling, she found that the first album started in 1897, and each succeeding one was a record of a holiday. Inside these albums was the life story of Mrs Gordon-Platt ... and, undoubtedly, Miss Beck. Miss Beck first appeared in the album dated 1904. This must have been the year after Mrs Gordon-Platt had come to Beacon Ride as a bride. Apparently Mrs Gordon-Platt had started compiling albums when she was about sixteen and in her holidaying she had visited most parts of the world. India, Germany, Norway, Sweden, France, Africa. On and on went the list of countries. Most of the albums started with a photograph of a ship. One was the *Orcades* of London, another was the *Strathnaver*. This one had taken her to India. Alison noted that there were only two albums dealing with the years following the first war and these were less exciting, showing places such as Torquay and the Isle of Wight.

The first snaps of Mrs Gordon-Platt showed a beautiful girl, then, as the dates on the albums got well into the new century, the pictures portrayed a handsome woman. In some of the albums family snaps had been inserted and Alison recognised Miss

Beck posing with two children, a good-looking boy and a plain-looking girl. The girl was undoubtedly Margaret, and the handsome young man her brother, the man whose double-dealing had set the pattern of Paul's life into one of struggle.

As Alison went through one album after another, covering most of the lifetime of Mrs Gordon-Platt, she gained an insight into the old lady's character. She would say now that Mrs Gordon-Platt the elder was a woman who had spared herself no luxury, whose whims had to be satisfied; and the thought came to Alison that had there not been so many whims, Beacon Ride would not be in such a dilapidated state as it was now.

Mrs Dickenson brought in tea and took it away again hardly touched, grumbling as was her wont. She came in finally to say she was going now and that she had left the supper ready, and Alison bade her good night as if speaking out of a dream.

She had even forgotten about Paul and the hurts of yesterday, until his sudden appearance startled her. And so engrossed was she in this old world that she greeted him as if they had parted in their usual friendly way that morning. Turning on her knees she cried, 'Paul! oh, Paul, come here. Come and look. You remember that lot with the old English cups? Well, I've made a find. I didn't know . . . I didn't know it then. Look!' She showed him the embossed writing-case and he stood looking down at it for a moment. Then his eyes coming to rest on her face, he asked, 'What's it all about?'

His voice sounded tired. He looked tired. She swung quickly to her feet, saying, 'Have you had any tea? Come and sit down, but be careful. Mind where you tread. I've something wonderful to tell you. It really is wonderful.' They were back on the old footing. He allowed her to press him into his chair, but when she said, 'I'll get you some tea,' he put in quickly, 'No, not tea. Give me a drink. Whisky.'

'Whisky? . . . Are you feeling all right?' Before he could answer she said, her voice rising, 'I told you. I told you you shouldn't go out. You'll be back where you started, if not further. I told you.'

'Give me a drink, Alison.' There was such a deflated tone to his voice that she turned quickly and poured him a drink. After he had finished it in one draught without even a shudder, he lay back in the armchair, and drawing in a deep breath said, 'That's better.' He put out his hand and patted her. 'You were quite right, Miss Read.' The corner of his mouth moved upwards. 'I did try to fly before I could walk. And it's bitter outside.' He drew in another breath and remained silent as he looked at her with a deep tenderness in his eyes, and then the expression was almost snapped away as he blinked and said briskly, 'Well, now I'm ready. What's your find?'

'Are you sure you're all right?'

'I'm ready for anything.' He hitched himself straighter in the chair, but she continued to look at him. His face was drawn, even haggard, and the worry that rose in her blotted out the excitement of the past hour.

'Come on.' His voice pushed her and she turned slowly towards the couch. Picking up the writing-case she held it out it to him, saying, 'It's this.'

He took it in his hands and after looking at the front turned it over and opened it. It was lined on both sides with blotting paper, which was almost obliterated with writing, which proved it had been used for its intended purpose. 'Yes, yes, I remember this lot . . . And those.' He pointed to the albums scattered on the floor, and the corner of his mouth moved further upwards as he went on, 'I remember thinking that if we accumulated much more of this stuff out back we'd better put a couple of shilling tables outside at the week-end. I said as much to Nelson and he said, why not? But I told him I wasn't going into partnership yet with Broadbent and Fowler.' He looked up at her now. 'Well, what about them? This' – he tapped the case – 'might bring a shilling or two if anybody wanted it, but it's cumbersome. It isn't a collector's piece, either.'

'If they knew what was inside it would be.'

'Inside of this?' He tapped the cover. 'What could

you get inside of this? What are you getting at, Alison?'

She dropped on her knees by his side and began hurriedly, 'You know when I first went up to Beacon Ride and I told you I thought I had seen the old people before, Mrs Gordon-Platt and her maid? Well, I had. They're there in those albums. But that isn't the point. Mrs Gordon-Platt was in a state because her cabinets had been sold while she was in hospital.' Alison did not mention Mrs Freda Gordon-Platt's name in connection with the cabinets. Something warned her against this. It also warned her not to mention the meeting with Miss Beck that very morning. So instead she said, 'When I saw Miss Beck she gave me a hint of what was in those cabinets and why Mrs Gordon-Platt was so upset at the loss of the albums.' Now Alison tapped the embossed cover of the writing-case. 'Apparently she had only one valuable piece of jewellery left . . . a necklace. And she broke it in two and put half in here.'

She watched Paul's puzzled expression as he repeated, 'In here?' Then he went on, 'She couldn't get anything in here.'

'Let's look and see. I didn't open it; I thought I would leave that to you. I'll get the stiletto.' She jumped up and, running to the mantelpiece, she took down a small, paper-thin blade. As she handed it to him she said with a laugh, 'You've managed to turn locks when keys have failed. There you are, have a go.'

Paul was examining the back thoroughly now, pressing, pushing. 'Did she say there was a spring?'

'No. She just said it took them quite a long while to insert the stones underneath these indents.' She pointed to the Prince of Wales's feathers and the crown.

Gently now Paul began to prise the cover from its base with the knife. After easing up one end, all he had to do was to insert his nail and lift off the thin brass cover. Slowly, he turned it over and laid it on his hands, then he stared at Alison in blank amazement before gazing down at the inside of the embossed writing-case again. There, lying in minute nests of cotton wool, was a tracery of chain and gems. The fine gold links of the necklace spread from one corner right across the inverted crown almost to the opposite corner. They had been placed in their little sockets like the pieces of a jigsaw puzzle.

'Good God!' The exclamation came from deep in his throat. 'The cunning old devil. Who would have believed it? And how mad to have put them in here.' Gently he lifted up a link of chain to reveal a stone rising out of its nest of cotton wool.

'Isn't it beautiful?' Alison gazed at the dangling stone.

'The old swine!'

Alison's head jerked upwards at the bitterness in Paul's voice. It was the first time she had heard him speak thus of any woman. Perhaps, she thought, with a touch of resentment, he considered the jewels belonged by right to Mrs Gordon-Platt's daughter-in-law. There was one thing certain: if Mrs Freda Gordon-Platt had just this half of the necklace, she wouldn't have to bother going round selling things ... not for a long while, anyway. She said quickly, 'She hid them for a purpose. They're for her daughter, Margaret.'

She almost fell backwards as Paul's knee jerked, and for a moment the writing-case was in danger of toppling on to the floor. As she steadied it with her hands she said quickly, 'Careful ... careful.'

'What do you know about Margaret?'

'Nothing. Well, just a bit.' She was stammering now. 'I know she married the gardener's son and her mother was upset at the time.' And she asked quietly, 'Did you know Margaret?'

There was a pause before he answered, 'Yes, I knew Margaret.' He was examining the tracery of gold chain and he spoke as if to the jewels. Enigmatically he said, 'It's damned unfair.'

'What do you mean, Paul? What's unfair?'

'Nothing ... nothing.' His voice was brusque and he moved uneasily in his chair, and added quickly, 'Now about these.' He tapped the necklace. 'Where do we stand? That's the point.'

'Where do we stand?' She was puzzled. 'We'll have to give them back to Mrs Gordon-Platt; we can't keep them.' She moved her head slowly. 'Of course we can't!'

'I don't know.'

'But, Paul!' Her voice was high. 'It's all she's got.'

'All she's got!' He almost spat the words out. 'She's had too much for too long, has Mrs Gordon-Platt. That's her trouble. I understood you to say that she wants her daughter to have these. Is that right?'

'Yes, that's what Miss Beck said.'

'Well, you never know with a woman like that. I think it would be wiser for us to keep them until the daughter turns up.'

Alison sat back on her heels and stared up at Paul. She couldn't believe it. She couldn't believe that Paul, the man who wouldn't get mixed up in any rings or questionable deals, should be talking in this way. He wanted to keep this find. Legally, she supposed, it belonged to him. Or did it? She would have to enquire; this was the first time the question had arisen.

Paul was now bending towards her, talking quietly, persuasively, 'Look, we won't do anything yet. The albums can be returned to the storeroom, but we'll keep this' – he tapped the writing-case – 'in a safe place.'

'No, Paul, please.'

At this point they heard the sound of the shop doorbell ringing, and as Alison wondered dazedly who it could be, Paul's head jerked to one side with sharp impatience as he exclaimed, 'That will be him, your Mr Roy.' There was undisguised bitterness in his voice, and now his hand came out and, gripping her shoulder, he said under his breath, 'Listen, Alison, listen to me. We'll do nothing about this matter until we've talked again. And don't mention it to anyone. Do you hear?'

'But, Paul . . .'

'Alison, I'm asking you to do something for me. Simply wait until we talk about this again. If he wasn't here now perhaps we could go on and discuss it, but he's at the door. Now look, go down and let him in. You can stall for a time; I'll leave that to you.' The corner of his mouth quivered.

She backed away from him and he said quietly to her now, 'Don't look at me like that, Alison.' When she did not answer he went on, 'Give me time to put these things away; he mustn't see them.'

Like someone walking in a dream, she turned away and went down the stairs. She couldn't believe what she knew to be true: Paul was meaning to keep this half of the necklace. Perhaps, as he had said, if they could have gone on talking he might have come to another decision about it. But would he? In her heart she doubted it. Oh, it would be the evening she had promised to go out, when she hadn't been out of an evening for weeks. She didn't know how she was going to get through it, for she would be able to think of nothing but Paul and that necklace.

But it wasn't Roy Gordon-Platt to whom she opened the door, it was Bill Tapley. 'Brr . . . rr!' He bustled past her, and as she closed the door slowly he asked, 'Paul in?'

'Yes . . . yes. But . . . but, I don't think he's up to much.'

'No? I thought he was getting along fine; he was out today. I just want a quick word with him.'

He was moving away now and she followed him up the shop, staring at his broad, thick shoulders as she said, 'I think he should be in bed.'

'Really?' He spoke over his shoulder. 'What's wrong with him now?'

'You know he had flu.' Her voice sounded indignant.

But his voice was mild as he replied, 'Yes. Yes, of course. But when I saw him at lunchtime in Eastbourne he looked as fit as a fiddle. Perhaps something he had for lunch didn't agree with him.'

'Did you have lunch with him?' There was a note of surprise in her tone.

'No, no.' They were at the staircase door now and he turned to her and bent towards her as he whispered, 'He was entertaining a lady-friend. I just happened to be in the hotel dining-room.'

She made a great effort not to let the impression

this news had made on her show on her face. Paul had been lunching with a woman in Eastbourne. She didn't have to guess twice at the woman's name. She felt anger rising in her again, and so consumed was she by it that she forgot that Paul had asked her to stall the visitor. She only remembered it as she preceded Bill Tapley into the drawing-room. It was when she saw Paul sitting on the couch calmly smoking that she thought, He must have moved like lightning to get that lot put away so quickly. She also noticed that Paul appeared surprised and not at all pleased to see who the visitor was, and his greeting reflected it.

Paul was on his feet now, and as he motioned the visitor to a chair, the shop bell rang once more. As Alison hurried out of the room, Bill Tapley laughingly said, 'Business seems good after hours,' and she thought, What is it about him that I can't stand? And why am I afraid of him? She hadn't realised until that moment that she was actually afraid of him.

She opened the shop door to the sight of Roy Gordon-Platt, dressed she thought, almost as if for a command performance. Sealock was, as its name suggested, a seaside town, and in or out of season no-one dressed to go to the Burley Hall unless it was for a mayoral occasion, and then only if you were a VIP in the front row of the circle. The thick fringe of her eyelashes flapped in perplexity for a moment, then she said as casually as she could, 'Hello. I'm sorry, but I'm not ready yet.'

He seemed slightly disappointed, but laughed lightly. 'We've got half an hour yet.'

'Half an hour!' She turned from him and hurried up the shop, talking over her shoulder as he followed. 'I won't be long. It doesn't take me long to get ready. I've been out all day and haven't long been back.'

'You sound tired. Are you sure you want to go out?' There was an anxious note in his voice as he followed her up the stairs.

'Oh, yes . . . yes. I'm looking forward to it.' And she was; she didn't want an evening in the company of Bill Tapley. And she was wondering at this moment what snappy comment Roy's appearance would draw from him.

She almost ran into the drawing-room as she exclaimed, 'Here's Roy, Paul. I'm late; I'll have to dash and get ready.' And she held out her arm towards Roy as if drawing him into the room.

Paul's expression gave nothing away as he looked at Roy, but Bill Tapley had trouble in controlling his grin.

She left them quickly, ran down to her room, and there changed into a dress she thought would not be too great a contrast to Roy's finery. It was a fine wool, powder blue with a cowl collar. She had never worn it before and was pleased with the effect. She had told herself that she was keeping this dress for an occasion. What occasion, she couldn't think. Well, she supposed this was an occasion, but whether it was worthy of a new dress was yet to be discovered.

Four hours later Alison could give herself the answer. Decidedly the occasion hadn't warranted the dress. True, Roy had done his best . . . poor boy. She thought of him as a boy, so much younger than herself, and this was really ridiculous, as she admitted when thinking about it. But he acted so much younger. Yet she knew she wasn't being fair to him, for she had compared his every move this evening with Paul. Paul was lovely to go out with. On the few occasions he had taken her out to dinner, things had glided. Paul knew what to do . . . Roy did too, but he worked too hard at it. This made him appear gauche. Apart from the Brahms *Academic Festival Overture*, without the help of the programme she couldn't have said what other item had been played, for although she had sat listening to the orchestra, her mind had been back in this house, going over the last few minutes with Paul before the doorbell had rung.

After the concert Roy had taken her to the Spa for a drink, and there in the lounge his youthfulness had embarrassed her, for he had indeed appeared a boy among men. If he had been dressed casually this wouldn't have been so apparent. He had the air, she thought, of an amateur London Johnnie at the beginning of the century. And so she was thankful when at last they reached the shop door. She did not ask him in but assured him that she had spent a wonderful evening. And he left her quite pleased with his efforts. She was able to shake her head at herself in the mirror, and smile and say, 'But he's a nice boy.'

She had expected Paul to be sitting up waiting for her, but all she found was a note that read, 'Gone to bed with a hot drink; see you in the morning. Goodnight.'

Later, lying in bed, her hands behind her head, out of all the events of an eventful day, her mind collected a thought, which she whispered aloud: 'What'll I do if he marries her?' And the answer unrolled itself in a series of pictures. She saw herself flitting from saleroom to saleroom, and buying the small pieces that would fit into her shop; she would have a shop, small and select, with a little flat above or at the back, and it would be exquisitely furnished. She saw herself in her flat of an evening sitting alone, working on her accounts. She saw herself lift up her face from the ledger and realised it was an old woman she was looking at. She took her hands from her head and with a barely audible groan turned on her side.

*   *   *

The following morning when she entered the kitchen it was to find Paul already up and about. He turned towards her, saying, 'Oh, I was just going to bring you some tea.'

'Why are you up? Are you feeling better?'

'Yes. Yes, I'm quite all right.'

She looked closely at him. He didn't look quite all right. He still had that peaked, drawn look that spoke of the aftermath of a bad bout of influenza. 'You should go away for a few days somewhere.'

He smiled wryly at her as he handed her the cup of tea, and then seating himself on the high stool near the breakfast table he slowly moved the spoon around the cup as he said, 'We could have a very nice holiday on that writing-case.'

'But Paul!' She sounded aghast, and as he clinked the spoon sharply on to the saucer, he put in quickly, 'All right, all right, I was only joking. What's the matter with you these days?'

'What's the matter with me!' Her eyes were wide, her eyebrows moving up. 'What's the matter with *me*?' she repeated. 'It's what's the matter with *you*!'

'Oh lord, Alison, don't let's start again, not at this time of morning. Although I'm feeling all right, I'm still not feeling all right at this time in the morning, you should know that by now.' The corner of his mouth quivered, but she would not answer the half-smile. She said sharply, 'You're not going to keep it, Paul, are you? You're going to give that half of the necklace—'

'Look, Alison.' With a deliberate movement he put his cup down on the table. 'I'm going to give it back, yes. It will reach its owner eventually . . . and I say eventually, but in the meantime I want you to leave it where it is . . . here.'

She could only stare at him. Paul Aylmer was known far beyond the precincts of his own town for fairness and squareness in a deal. He was looked upon by many in the trade as a prig, but that hadn't deterred him from doing what he thought was right. Yet at this moment she did not believe him when he said that the stones would eventually reach their rightful owner. She felt that for some reason he was intent on keeping them. But why? As far as she knew he wasn't hard up, and even if he had been, there was her money. Then it came to her that she had the reason why he wanted to hang on to this half of the necklace. If the stones were returned to Mrs Gordon-Platt it was almost a certainty that Freda Gordon-Platt would never see them. She thought bitterly, She's a fast worker, I'll say that for her. In three days she had wiped out the bitterness of twenty years and so enlisted his sympathy that he was back almost where he had been. She recalled to mind Nelson's remark about his love for Freda . . . stark, staring mad. And this caused her voice to reach a cracked, high note as she exclaimed, 'That writing-case belongs to old Mrs Gordon-Platt and she should have it immediately. You know she should.'

'All right.' He was facing her now, his tone almost a growl. 'Take her the writing-case by all means, but the contents stay here, and that's my last word on it.'

For one moment longer he glared at her, then jerking the cord of his dressing-gown tightly round his waist he turned away and marched out of the room.

She stood with her fingers pressed tightly against her lips. She had a great desire to flop down and howl. Never before had Paul spoken to her like that. She shook her head to prevent the tears coming and exclaimed aloud, 'That beastly woman!'

Four

ALISON ALWAYS THOUGHT OF THE WEEK THAT followed as the lead-up to the day of . . . THE SALE, the sale that acted as a gun to shoot her world into fragments.

After Paul had said plainly that he meant to keep the find in the writing-case, he refused to allow her to bring up the subject again. Following the testy conversation over that early morning cup of tea, she had tried to approach him and he had allowed her to go on for a time, then had answered her quietly and briefly, saying, 'Alison, trust me in this.'

She wanted to, oh, she wanted to trust him, but she knew she couldn't, and when on the Saturday morning she again opened the subject he turned on her fiercely, and speaking emphatically, cried, 'If you don't give me time, I swear that old woman won't see her precious stones again, and I mean it.' And Alison knew him well enough to know he did mean it. She became swamped in a feeling of apprehension, which did not lessen when there came into the shop at half-past eleven on Saturday morning, a visitor . . . not a customer. It was Mrs Freda Gordon-Platt.

Before she could speak, Alison said, 'I'm afraid Paul isn't here.' She couldn't keep the coolness from her tone.

Mrs Freda Gordon-Platt looked at her for a long moment; then smiling stiffly she remarked, 'Oh, I've missed him, then.'

'Had you an appointment?' Alison's tone was strictly businesslike and, she knew, very much out of place. It caused a ripple of humour to pass over Mrs Freda Gordon-Platt's face and her head went slightly to the side as she said, 'Yes, I had an appointment.' She stressed the word appointment. 'When we spoke on the phone this morning I—'

'Well, perhaps he's forgotten,' Alison cut in rudely.

'I don't think so.' Now the chin came in and the patient tone was such as one uses to an erring child, or a young girl at best: 'You are very fond of Paul, aren't you, my dear?'

'I don't see what that's got to do with it.'

'Don't you? I think you do. And I can understand

it. He's a person one can get very fond of, very fond—'

'It's taken a long time for you to find it out. It's a pity you didn't think that way years ago.'

'What do you know about my business?' Mrs Freda Gordon-Platt's face looked thin and pinched now, and at that moment there was the definite stamp of forty on her features.

'Quite a bit.' They stood looking at each other in what could only be called a hate-filled silence, and it was the older woman who regained her composure first. She actually smiled at Alison, and shaking her head and in a tone that spoke of understanding, she said, 'Youth. Oh, youth. Well, we all have to be young; it's a penalty, and we all have to learn, haven't we? And while I'm on about youth, my son, at the moment, is wallowing in one of youth's traps . . . He has fallen in love with you.'

'That's nonsense; we've only met three times.'

'It can happen in the first minute, I've heard. Anyway, there it is. And let me tell you, my son is a nice boy.'

'I have found that out already for myself . . . and I can't understand—'

'Please don't say it.' Freda Gordon-Platt's voice was sharp and her hand was suddenly raised. 'Don't you dare say you don't know how it came about he is my son.'

Alison stared at the woman in genuine surprise. 'I had no intention of making such a trite remark. I was merely about to say that I don't understand how he could tell you that. After all, he was only out once with me.'

'He did not tell me. I'm his mother and I happen to know him. And I would like to inform you at this point —' Mrs Gordon-Platt drew herself to her full height of five-feet ten before going on, 'that you'd be a very fortunate girl if you got my boy. . . . But just how fortunate he would be, only the years ahead would tell.'

After this slap, Alison was about to return when she was stopped once again with an imperious lift of the hand. 'I don't wish to haggle with you, my dear; I'm going. And when Paul comes back, tell him I called and have gone on to The Crown.'

As Alison watched the woman sail out of the shop there was no anger left within her. She was no longer bristling with indignation but deflated, utterly deflated. Mrs Freda Gordon-Platt's last words had achieved this. They gave confirmation that Paul and she were meeting . . . 'I've gone on to The Crown.'

Nelson came out of the back shop at this point, and looking along the length of the drugget towards the door, he remarked, 'There'll be trouble. Aa can feel it in the air. It's as if we was back in the old days' . . .

At around one o'clock on that Saturday Miss Beck

phoned, and the mere sound of her voice had brought a feeling of acute guilt to Alison. Although at this stage she could tell her truthfully that she had not found the tea-caddy but was still looking, and hoping, there was a hint of tears in Miss Beck's voice as she rang off. And they wouldn't have been there, Alison knew, if she could have told her that at least half her troubles were over, for she had found the writing-case.

The week-end passed like a nightmare. It seemed endless, at times unreal; at other moments it seemed to be a pattern of all her life ahead.

Tuesday was the day of the sale. Paul had said to her, 'I'll be away for the day. I've marked the items I'd like you to try for; I'd particularly like the French repeater carriage clock. Also the Victorian four-drawer Davenport.'

In reply she had said, 'Are you going to be away all day?'

'Yes.' He was straining his neck and adjusting his tie in the mirror above the mantelpiece, and for a fleeting second he looked at her reflection in the glass before lowering his head and saying, in a gentle tone, 'Keep tomorrow free, will you, Alison? I would like you to come over to Eastbourne with me.'

'Eastbourne?' Her heart gave a jump.

'Yes. It's to do with the business of the writing-case.' He turned his head slowly and they looked at each other for a moment in silence before she burst out, 'You're not selling the stones?' She watched him close his eyes for a moment and his head drooped again before he said patiently, 'I'm not selling the stones; I'll explain everything to you tomorrow.'

Instead of feeling relieved she felt more weighed down with apprehension, if that were possible. There was something . . . well, something fishy about Paul's manner and behaviour, to say the least.

The sale started at eleven. It was not an important sale. There were no big dealers present; the local ones who were there sat together at the back of the room. Alison managed to get her usual seat near the rostrum, but to reach it she had to pass behind a low partition of furniture, where the men gathered. At the end of the partition stood Bill Tapley, talking to another dealer, but he turned his head quickly as she passed and smiled at her, and she had hardly seated herself before he was bending above her, saying, 'Hello, Alison; any room for a little 'un?' Without waiting for a response he squeezed past her and into the empty chair next to hers. 'After anything special?' He leant towards her.

'Nothing much,' she replied without turning her head. 'Just the Davenport and the French carriage clock.'

It was quite usual for dealers to discuss what they meant to bid for, so that they wouldn't inadvertently push the price up for each other. If more than one of them wanted the same piece, they might amicably decide who was to have it, and it was no new thing to see money changing hands and dealers buying from each other after the sale. At the same time, they also might fight each other at the bidding for it. Yet, like birds of a feather, they usually flew in the one direction, so it was not unusual that Alison should tell Bill Tapley what she was bidding for.

The clock struck eleven as the auctioneer took the stand, and being in a jovial mood this morning he started with, 'Now, gentlemen, let us have no dilly-dallying or shilly-shallying during the next hour or so. It's your money I'm after and as you've kindly come here to give it to me, don't hesitate to hand it over . . . Lot one, a convex mirror in gilt frame. What am I bid? Ten shillings? . . . Ten, twelve, fourteen, sixteen . . .'

And so it went on for the next half-hour. At lot fifty-four the Davenport came up. Alison bid up to £18 and as it went to a private buyer for £22, Bill Tapley muttered under his breath, 'Blasted fool! It's the likes of him that would bring you down to tea and dripping.' He laughed at his own joke, and looking sideways at Alison, said, 'Sorry you didn't get it. It was a nice piece. That fellow likely knew what he was after.'

The French clock was lot eighty-four. But following

seventy, the auctioneer paused and said, 'We've a written-in lot here; it's on the table, there. Some nice pieces, very nice. Come on, you china addicts and get bidding for this Sèvres . . . Yes' – he nodded his head around the room – 'two nice pieces of Sèvres there, not to mention bits of Doulton and a nice specimen of a Regency tea-caddy.'

The auctioneer's words brought Alison to the edge of her chair, then on to her feet. She looked over the three rows of people in front of her towards the long table that flanked the rostrum. The porter was holding up a beautifully inlaid tea-caddy. He lifted the lid, closed it again, then picked up the plates one at a time to show them round the room. As she gazed almost spellbound towards him, one or two people left their seats and moved forward towards the table; but Alison sat down. Her legs felt weak beneath her. She had searched Eastbourne, Brighton, Bexhill and Hastings and here on her very doorstep were the items she was looking for, among them Miss Beck's tea-caddy. As always when excited she shivered, then started as Bill Tapley said quietly, 'Nice little lot, that. Usually reserved for the upper floor and the upper crust, that kind of stuff. I think I'll try for it myself.' She turned quickly to look at him and something in her expression caused him to say, 'Any objection?'

She shook her head briefly but did not speak. It would just have to happen that she was sitting next to Bill Tapley and that he would decide to bid for this particular lot.

'Well, what'll I start them at, gentlemen?'

When silence greeted this remark, as was often the way when a number of people were interested in a certain lot, the auctioneer said brusquely, 'Now, come along, come along, don't stall. Don't tell me that this isn't an interesting little lot. What am I offered? Eh? . . . Thank you, sir. One pound bid, twenty-five, thirty, thirty-five. Two pounds, two pounds-five.'

Alison was stiff with tension. She would let them go on and when they stopped she would start. But she knew that Bill Tapley would start also. She could have cried with vexation.

'Five pounds-ten.' The auctioneer sent his shrewd gaze over the crowd. 'Five pounds-ten, ladies and gentlemen. Somebody's going to get a very cheap lot; a gift, I should say. . . . Five pounds-ten.'

Alison moved her pencil and the auctioneer said, 'Five-fifteen,' then went on, 'six pounds, six pounds-five, six pounds-ten, six pounds-fifteen, seven pounds, . . . seven pounds.' He paused and the pause was in Alison's favour, then a hidden bidder from the back of the room must have joined the fray, for the auctioneer now said, 'Seven-five . . . seven-ten, seven-fifteen, eight pounds, eight-five, eight-ten, eight-fifteen. Eight-fifteen,' he repeated. The hammer wavered, and as Alison waited for it to drop gently on the desk, she thought that Bill Tapley, aiming to curry her favour, was going to let her have this lot. For the briefest second she felt grateful to him, then the auctioneer's eyes moved just the slightest and he smiled as he took Bill Tapley's bid and went on, 'Eight-fifteen, nine pounds. Here we go again, nine pounds, nine-five, nine-ten, nine-fifteen, ten pounds.' Alison was beginning to feel desperate. He was pushing her up, and up and up. She could feel he was enjoying this battle of bids, and wills. Not only had he taken a fancy to the lot but if he could beat her on this he would undoubtedly take it as an omen. The lot was now jumping in ten-shilling bids and when it reached £18 she thought wildly, I'll go to thirty. I must; I'll go to thirty. But before they had outbidded each other to £25 the auctioneer paused and the room became so still that it could have been empty of people. It was doubtful whether the regular buyers in the saleroom had previously come across anything so intense and exciting as this incident. Here were two dealers fighting it out. Sitting next to each other, their eyes riveted on the auctioneer, they were fighting it out. But now the auctioneer said, 'That tea-caddy there. Fred, hand it up.' When the caddy was in his hand he examined it thoroughly and when he opened it he exclaimed, 'Yes, very nice, very nice indeed. Glass liner still intact, a beautifully preserved piece, but it isn't made of gold or silver, and as far as I can speak in my small experience'

– there was a titter at this – 'I've never known a tea-caddy to have a secret drawer.' As he tapped each side and the bottom of the caddy the titter increased. It spread over the whole room, but it evoked no murmur from either Alison or Bill Tapley.

The auctioneer, now handing the tea-caddy back to the porter, looked down at Alison, and smiling, said briefly, 'Ready?' There was another wave of muted laughter as she moved her pencil once more.

When Bill Tapley had bid £30 a dealer moving from the crowd went to the table, and lifting one of the plates turned it over and examined it. This brought a curt reprimand from the auctioneer. 'Would you mind remaining quiet during the bidding, sir? There was plenty of time to examine the pieces before the sale started.'

The buyer shrugged off the reprimand and returned to his place, and once more the bidding was in progress. 'Thirty pounds, ten shillings, thirty-one pounds.' The auctioneer's head became like a pendulum as he confirmed each bid. 'Thirty-seven pounds.' It was Bill Tapley's bid. She paused and looked down. If only Paul were here; if only she could be sure that if she went to forty, Bill Tapley would drop out. She was aware of the tension in the saleroom pressing on her, acting like a tight band around her head. They all knew that this was just an ordinary sale where a single lot might reach £25, or £30 at the most. It was only at the monthly sales on the first floor where the prices reached the £50, the £100 and the £200 mark. She made a quick decision. She would go up to £50. Even if Miss Beck couldn't pay, she herself would put up the rest. What was in that tea-caddy was worth more than £50.

When Alison bid £50 the auctioneer stopped and began to write something on a piece of paper. There was a rustle of curiosity in the room as he beckoned a porter and whispered as he handed the note to him. The porter now brought the piece of folded paper to Alison. Opening it, whilst keeping it shielded with one hand, she read the spidery words, 'Does Paul know? If Tapley is set on this, he'll go the limit.'

She folded the paper quickly and pushed it into her pocket. She felt quite unnerved. Yet she moved her pencil once again. At £56 pounds the auctioneer said tensely, 'This is nonsensical, to say the least. It's becoming a private battle. This lot has gone far beyond its worth; you know that, Mr Tapley.'

'I'm still bidding.' Bill Tapley's voice was quiet and unemotional and it had the power to take the last ounce of fight out of Alison. She thought wildly, I can't go on, I'll bargain with him after. She lowered her hand with the pencil in it and when it dropped across her knee the auctioneer said, 'The bidding stands at fifty-six pounds.' He paused a moment and looked from Alison's bent head to Bill Tapley's unblinking eyes, then dropped the ivory mallet.

An audible sigh, like a breaking wave, swept over the room. Alison knew that all eyes were turned in her direction. As she kept looking down at her catalogue and pretended to be writing, she was conscious of Bill Tapley sitting smugly back in the chair beside her. She felt it impossible to remain near him a moment longer, but forced herself to stay until the bidding got into sway once more so that her departure would not cause so much comment. As she gathered up her bag and gloves, Bill Tapley said quietly, 'We'll talk about it later, if you like.' She moved her head in his direction but she could not trust herself to look at him. Without giving him any answer she rose and walked the gauntlet of all eyes until she was in the street.

Ten minutes later she entered the drawing-room, and without taking off her outdoor things she dropped on to the couch. Pressing her face into the corner, slowly and painfully she began to cry.

A minute or so later Nellie's voice startled her by saying, 'You all right, Miss Alison?'

She sniffed and blew her nose, then smiling weakly up at Mrs Dickenson, she said, 'I've got a dose of the blues, Nellie.'

'Oh, blues! I thought something had happened. Well, if you've got the blues, miss, there's only one cure for that, and that's work.' She moved her compact body to give this fact stress. 'I know what the blues is and I say to meself, get going, Nellie Dickenson, get going.'

'Yes, Nellie, you're right.'

'Shall I make you a cup of tea? Lunch will be another half-hour or so.'

'Yes, thank you very much, Nellie.'

As Mrs Dickenson turned away, the telephone bell rang and she said flatly, 'Don't disturb yourself, I'll see to it.'

Within a minute she had put her head round the door again, whispering, 'It's for you.'

The voice that greeted her over the phone was that of Bill Tapley, and she was definitely surprised to hear it, for she thought he would have left the next move to her; also that he would have stayed until the end of the sale. His voice held a tinge of laughter as he said, 'How are you feeling now? A bit battle-scarred?'

'No,' she lied glibly, 'these things happen. All I can say is that you must have wanted that lot badly.'

'No. No, I didn't want it all that much. I just wanted to beat you.'

She brought her teeth together as she looked down into the mouthpiece. 'And now I suppose you want to make a deal with me, putting a hundred per cent on at the very least, is that it?'

'Not necessarily. I'm prepared to give you the lot. What's sixty pounds?' He laughed here. 'I think we'd better have a chat, eh? Like to come round?'

She moved her eyes quickly from one side of the hall to the other as if searching for guidance. She had never been in Bill Tapley's house, although she had passed it many times. It looked a nice house, one of a Regency block, and recently he'd had it done up. In an ordinary way she would have answered this invitation with, What's wrong with you coming to the shop? but this was something that she had to deal with alone, without Nelson listening in the background . . . or Paul putting in an unexpected appearance. That was the last thing she wanted. She hadn't decided yet how she would explain to him about the episode in the saleroom, for he was nearly sure to hear of it; the dealers would naturally think she was buying for him. She asked abruptly now, 'When?'

'No time like the present, is there? I've just got in and I'm having a drink. If you come straight along you can join me.'

'Very well.'

'That's settled, then.'

She put down the receiver; then going to the kitchen she said to Mrs Dickenson, 'I've got to go out. Sorry about the tea; I'll be about half an hour, Nellie.'

'Oh! well, don't be longer, mind; lunch won't improve with keeping.'

She was down the stairs before Mrs Dickenson finished speaking. In the shop she evaded Nelson's enquiry of 'Did you get anything this mornin'? Aa didn't see you come in; you were quick back.'

'I'll tell you about it later, Nelson; I won't be long.'

As she reached the green-painted door and lifted her hand to the brass knocker she said to herself, Go easy, don't get his back up.

He could have been waiting behind the door, so quickly did he answer her knock. He was not profuse in his greeting, saying simply, 'You weren't long. Come in.'

When she stepped into the hall the first thing that drew her attention was the quality of the few pieces standing against the walls, and when she entered the sitting-room she was more than surprised to see with what taste the room was arranged. It was also the room of a collector, not a seller. She had always imagined that Bill Tapley would sell anything for money. She was forced to remember that when she had first seen Paul's rooms they held nothing like the pieces that graced this apartment.

If Bill Tapley noticed her interest he made no comment, but going to a cocktail cabinet that stood in the corner, illuminated by interior lighting, he lifted up a glass already full of sherry and brought it to her. 'This is an occasion,' he said.

She did not answer him, but as he inclined his own glass towards her she made a slight motion with her head before sipping at the sherry. 'There now' – he was smiling his wide grin – 'our first drink together. I hope it won't be our last. But come, sit down.'

The chair she sat on, and others dotted about the

room, were in the Louis Quatorze style, and she was irritated with herself for being impressed by this unexpected side to him, and the elegance with which he surrounded himself. She wouldn't have believed it without seeing it for herself, for judging by his outward appearance he was a coarse individual. She would never have given him credit for good taste in anything. But he undoubtedly had taste. The glass she was drinking out of was, she imagined, a collector's piece in itself. She was brought to the reason for her visit by him saying, 'Well now, Alison, you want to do business? But first of all, tell me why were you so eager to get that lot?'

'I . . . I had an interested buyer.'

'And he was prepared to go up to fifty for it? I can't see why. I've examined the caddy. It's really nothing; I've seen dozens better. It'll bring about four pounds . . . not more, and as Renault said, there're no secret panels.'

Alison drew in a deep breath, then said, 'It's of sentimental value. It's been in a particular family for years.'

'Which family? Why did they sell it, then?'

She leant forward now as if confiding in him, and her voice dropped a tone as she said, 'The Gordon-Platts.'

She watched him press himself back into the curve of the chair. She watched his face screw up and his eyes peer at her; and his lower lip protruded just the slightest with a scornful tilt as he brought out, 'Oh, Alison, Alison. Come clean. I know those things came from the Gordon-Platts. Renault himself told me who had put them in. It was the young Mrs Gordon-Platt who, perhaps you may know, was once very interested in Paul. Or didn't you know that?'

She was sitting stiffly now. 'Yes. Yes, I know all about it. But it's the elder Mrs Gordon-Platt who wants the things.' Alison thought it unwise to go into any further detail here, for the slightest mistake on her part and he would become suspicious.

He said now, 'The elder Mrs Gordon-Platt? But I thought she was harder up than all the church mice put together.'

'You seem to know a great deal about them.'

'Yes. Yes, I am pretty well informed about most things. It would surprise you the things I know.' He nodded his head at her in a peculiar way, then added, 'Come along, drink up and let me refill your glass.'

'No, thanks. I won't have another . . . Now, about the lot.' She tried to speak with a cool, businesslike air. 'What will you take for it?' As he began to smile she put in quietly, 'You had your fun in the saleroom, but now it's over, so let's get down to business.'

He lifted his chin, pushing his head back on to the rim of the chair, but his eyes were still slanted down on to her as he said, 'What if my price is too high?'

'You haven't named it . . . Name it.'

'You.'

She felt the blood rushing to her face; her whole body became hot; but it was no use, she knew, being evasive and saying, 'What do you mean?' She knew what he meant and he knew that she knew. She looked down into the glass and swirled the remainder of her sherry around it as she said, 'You have a poor estimation of my value. I thought I was worth a little more than fifty-five pounds . . . plus interest.'

'You are.' He brought his thick head and shoulders towards her. 'That will be a mere pinprick to what I'll give you. You know, Alison, it's not widely known, but I can say in all modesty I'm not exactly a poor man; my father saw to that. But what I have is yours for the taking.' His hand came out and his fingers rested gently on the point of her knee. She did not move from his touch as he went on, his voice low and slightly thick now, 'From the moment I saw you in Paul's shop . . . you were only a child then, but I knew as far back as that morning that I would want to marry you. They can say lots of things about me in this town, but never that I've chased after women. No. I've got my standards, although I know that you don't give me credit for such things as standards; but I've waited long and patiently. Look around this room.' Which he proceeded to do, forcing her to follow his gaze. 'Since I took over the business, I've collected a lot of beautiful things around me ... I like beauty ... Even if it holds a little spitfire.' He laughed and pressed his fingers into her knee.

Still not moving, she said, 'And you want to collect me?'

'No, no; I don't want to *collect* you. I want to give you what I've collected. I want you to marry me.'

Alison was amazed at her feelings at this moment, because they were not antagonistic towards him. Very few women, she realised, were capable of hating a man who was offering them marriage, and her own feelings were definitely modified now. She felt sorry for him in a way; she felt she even liked him. She had misjudged him about many things, she thought, and had never given him credit for finer feelings, so her voice had a note of regret in it when she said, 'I'm sorry, Bill, really I am, but it's no use. You see ... well, the vital thing's missing, I don't happen to love you.'

His fingers moved from her knee and he clasped his hands together and surveyed them as he said, 'That will come.'

'I'm afraid not; in fact, I'm sure it wouldn't.' She shook her head and then repeated, 'It wouldn't be any use ... because, well, I ...' She fumbled to a stop, knowing she couldn't go on and tell him the truth.

He was staring at her again. 'You were going to say something; you were going to tell me why you couldn't love me.' He waited and when she didn't answer he said, 'You're in love with somebody else, aren't you?' She stared at him unblinking, making no move whatever as he went on very softly, 'You're beating your head against a brick wall, you know.'

'I don't understand.'

'I think you do. You're in love with Paul, aren't you? At least, you think you are.' His voice was still low. 'My idea is that you're mixing up gratitude with love and you can't see the difference between the two emotions. But even if you were really in love with him, he isn't in love with you . . . and never could be.'

She was sitting stiff again, back on the old footing, and she demanded now, 'How do you know? You know nothing at all about it.'

'I *do* know something about it. In fact, I know a great deal about it. I know that Paul isn't in love with you because he's in love with somebody else.'

'He isn't.' She felt like a child hitting back with the first thing, the obvious thing, that came to mind. 'It's only because she knew him years ago. How can he still be in love with her, when she ran off and left him? If you know so much about everything, you'll know that.'

He threw his head up with a jerk, saying now, 'Oh, her! You mean Freda? I wasn't referring to her. But she's another one; she doesn't know either that she's kicking at a brick wall. No, Alison, your dear Paul, I'm sorry to have to inform you, has a woman in Eastbourne. He's had her for years. I don't feel any compunction in telling you this, for it's about time your idol was shattered. I've thought so for a long time. This woman has a family and a husband somewhere. He goes off for long periods and that's all I know about him. But I do know that Paul visits her regularly and that the children adore him. Make what you like out of that.'

'You're lying! You're making it up!' She was on her feet now, standing over him, glaring down at his bent head. 'Paul keeping a woman! You know, Bill Tapley, you're a wicked, spiteful devil. . . . You're a . . . o-oh!'

'Okay, I'm a wicked, spiteful devil. Would you repeat that if I give you proof?'

'I'd never believe it, for you couldn't prove it, I know you couldn't. It's just men's talk . . . You're . . . You're . . .'

'Look here, Alison.' The kindly manner had disappeared now and Bill Tapley's face was grim; and his voice matched it as he said, 'It's sickened me to see you glorifying him as if he were a god, and all the while he was running another house on the side. But I said to myself, well, it's his business . . . and now I'm saying to you that it is his business. If he wants to run a woman and have a family on the side, that's his business. Even when he's doing it behind another fellow's back, it's still his business. It only becomes *my* business when the girl I want to marry holds him up to me as a paragon . . . Then it sticks in my gullet.'

'You've never liked Paul, have you?' Alison's voice was calm now.

'No. He's too damned uppish for my taste; too much of the square-deal boy. But I could have stomached that if it hadn't been for this other business.'

'I don't believe you. I don't believe this other business. Paul would never . . .'

'Has it ever struck you that he goes to Eastbourne every Wednesday and stays there all day, and sometimes on a Monday, too?'

'What's wrong in going to Eastbourne as many times a week as he likes?'

'Come off it, Alison, face up to it. I've seen the house that he runs. I came across it by accident; it's a smallholding on the outskirts. I was taking a short cut one day and there he was saying goodbye to a woman at the gate. There were only three children around him then; last year there were four. This has been going on for a long time. Whenever I'm going through, I take that road, just to see. Then, as recently as last Wednesday, I saw him having lunch with her in The Bells; I went across purposely. He brazened it out but she turned her face away . . . right away. Look, I'll take you to the place. This is Tuesday, isn't it? I bet you what you like he's there at this minute. There's a main road cuts right by, and a wood on the other side

. . . Look.' He had her by the shoulders. 'You'll never get over this infatuation until you're convinced that it's no use hanging on. He's been a father to you, and that's what he'll remain, nothing more . . . If I can prove this to you, will you give me a chance? That's all I ask; I won't rush it, but just give me a chance. Come on, come on over to Eastbourne now. We may see him or we may not, but come and see.'

'No. No, I won't come. No.'

'You're afraid, aren't you? You know what I've said is true, every word of it. You've only to put two and two together.'

'I don't believe it. I tell you, I don't. There's some mistake.'

'Look, Alison, I'll make a deal with you. You come over to Eastbourne with me and I'll let you have that lot for what I paid for it. What about it? There it is. I'll ring the saleroom this minute and tell Renault, and you can give him the cheque. What about it?'

As her head drooped she gripped the back of the chair to steady herself: she knew that even without this offer she would eventually have agreed to go with him to Eastbourne. She would have to know the truth. She would have to see for herself.

Her whisper was almost inaudible, but he heard it and went to the phone. And when he came back he said, 'It's all right. Renault's transferring it; it's yours. Now, would you like a bite of lunch before we set off?'

'No, thanks.' She felt faint, even ill. As Bill Tapley had prophesied, she was going back in her mind over Paul's movements during the past years. Regularly he had made a trip to Eastbourne on a Wednesday, and always by himself. Paul had another home, and a woman, and children . . . Perhaps it had happened before she came on the scene years ago. She literally shook herself as she realised she was already accepting what Bill Tapley had said as gospel truth. He appeared at her side now with his coat on and when he put his arm about her shoulders as they went towards the door she stiffened and shrank inwardly from his touch. And she knew that he was not unaware of this, but he still kept his arm round her shoulders . . .

They hardly exchanged a word on the journey to Eastbourne, but when they had passed through the town and turned off the main road into a winding lane he said, 'Well, we're almost there. We may have to sit it out and even then see nothing for our pains . . . at least, I'd better qualify that, hadn't I?' He gave a grim laugh. 'My pains. There's the house.'

Alison turned her head swiftly and looked over a stretch of grass, boarded by chestnut fencing, towards a bungalow. It looked as uninteresting as a square box. To the right of it stood a portable garage and a number of outhouses, and to the left a row of greenhouses with some cultivated fields beyond. It was, as he had said, a smallholding. She was puzzled and bewildered beyond her depth.

A short distance along the road, and before they came to the end of the chestnut palings surrounding the land belonging to the bungalow, Bill Tapley turned the car across a rutted path and into the wood opposite. He had evidently been here before, for with an agility born of practice he swung the car this way and that between the trees and eventually brought it round again to face the road, slanting in the direction of the gate that led to the house. After he had stopped the engine he sat back and lit a cigarette before speaking. 'It might be a long wait; it's only ten minutes to three. Would you like to get out and stroll through the wood? You can keep the house in view.'

'No, thanks, I'll wait here . . .'

At half-past three they were still waiting. He had broken the silence now and again but merely to make a remark that did not require an answer. It was quarter to four when he said, 'I should have brought a flask of tea,' and then pulling the glove-box lid down he added, 'There should be some chocolate in here somewhere.' He was leaning back against the seat now with a bar of chocolate in his hand when his arm suddenly shot out and, pushing Alison sharply, he whispered, 'Duck down.'

She did not enquire why she had to do this but

immediately bent her head. Then turning sideways she whispered, 'What is it?'

Bill Tapley twisted round, his face turned from the windscreen, and, pretending to be reaching into the back seat, he said, 'Paul. He's in the field over there.' The statement was like the jab of a needle deep into her body. She closed her eyes against the pain of it, and when she opened them again Bill Tapley was sitting once more in his seat facing the front but with his head down. He whispered, 'He's just gone past, but take a look.'

Slowly and very reluctantly Alison lifted her head, then moved it to one side to get a better view of the figure walking in the field across the road. And although it was some distance away, she had no difficulty in recognising Paul. His height, his breadth, the lift of his head, the way he walked, were as much a part of her as her own personality. That was Paul, Paul in his shirtsleeves, his hair ruffled. Paul wearing wellington boots, Paul carrying a pail in each hand. Paul accompanied by two children, both under school age. The needle went deeper when, through the open window she heard the shrill cries of the children. After Paul had disappeared from view she drooped her head and closed her eyes. And when Bill Tapley's hand covered hers, she did not pull it away. She had never liked Bill Tapley, considering him inferior in all ways to Paul. There had been rumours that some of his business methods wouldn't bear too close an inspection and she hadn't been at all surprised to hear this. But she had condemned him, mainly because he fell far short of the man she thought she knew.

Like everyone else, she read the Sunday papers, read of people leading double lives. But she knew that this kind of thing only happened to other people, to unreal people, not to people with whom you lived . . . Not Paul. Bill Tapley was saying, 'We'd better wait a while; they'll be back in a minute.' And he was right. In a few minutes the children came across the field, and again she bent her head, but not so far this time; she felt it didn't matter if he saw her or not. Nothing mattered any more.

She slowly straightened as Bill Tapley said, 'They've gone indoors.' And turning fully to her he took both her hands in his, saying, 'I'm sorry, you know; I had to do this. I've never liked squeaking on anyone, not even Paul, and I must admit, as I've already told you, I've never had much love for him. And while I'm on, I'd better tell you something else. Give it to you in one blow, so to speak. You've always thought that my main interest in you was because, in a few months' time, you'll come into a tidy sum . . . Now' – he shook her hands – 'don't deny it, I know it's true. And on my part I won't deny that I don't despise money. Oh, no. Only a fool despises money. A wise man makes it, and uses it. I'm a wise man like my father before me. But if money was my only interest in you then I'd have dropped any thought of you a long time ago, because, Alison' – he paused and waited for her eyes to come to his – 'what I'm going to tell you now is going to be a bit of a shock, but, I repeat, you might as well have it altogether . . . Well, the truth is, I don't think you have any money to come into.'

'No? No money to come into? What do you mean? I had eighteen thousand, and it's been invested.'

'Paul is the sole trustee, isn't he?'

'Yes. Yes, he is.'

'And you've never bothered to ask him what's happening to your money?'

'No; no, of course not.'

'Well. I'll tell you what's happened to it. Years ago, Paul got himself into a jam. It was through the man that Freda Carter married, Charles Gordon-Platt. Funny how that name keeps cropping up.' He nodded his head now. 'Paul had to carry the can for him. Now, before this happened, Paul's old man died and my father offered to buy the business, but Paul was a big-head then and showed my father the door in no uncertain terms. Well, comes the blow-up. Charles Gordon-Platt does a bunk and leaves Paul in the soup. They had taken over a printing business and gathered enough debts to choke a big company, let alone a couple of fellows. Paul was in up to his neck to the tune of nineteen thousand pounds . . . Yes' –

he nodded at her – 'all there was for it was to go bankrupt, and he didn't want to do that, because the only way he could hope to get on his feet again was to keep the business going, and you know you can't start a business as an undischarged bankrupt. Well, he comes to my father . . . crawling now, and my father, being a businessman, does a deal with him. He lends him twenty thousand at a certain per cent, with the house standing as part security . . . a very small part, as property was at a low ebb then. Well, Paul could just about manage the interest, and had to scrape like mad to do it, until you came on the scene . . . Oh! You were a gift from the Gods, for presto! my father received sixteen thousand down on the nail, and two years later the other four. And you can't tell me that in the last eight years Paul's made your eighteen thousand in profit from the business, plus interest on the eighteen thousand, plus again the cost of running two homes. No, whatever Paul's made it doesn't run into thousands, unless he's learned some business tricks that I don't know about . . . Now, don't look so shocked. It's better that you learn everything in one fell swoop, isn't it? It's the only way to cure you, as I can see.' She turned away from his eyes and stared out through the windscreen again. She felt numbed; not shocked about this latest piece of news, just numbed. She remembered she had said to Paul just a day or so ago, 'You want it all ways.' She

hadn't realised how many ways he did want it . . .
and was actually having it . . . Yet it was strange,
but if using her money was the only thing Paul had
to answer for, then there would have been no issue
at all. And she knew now why he wanted to keep the
necklace. It wasn't for Mrs Freda Gordon-Platt. Yet
this fact brought her no ease, for even the significance
of Mrs Freda Gordon-Platt faded before the proof of
the bungalow. She turned her head and leaned out
of the open window so as to get more air, and Bill
Tapley, moving closer to her, put his arm around her
saying, 'There, there; don't take it so badly.'

She kept drawing in great gulps of air. She felt sick;
literally, she could be sick. He turned her round and
pressed her against the seat, saying soothingly, 'Look;
I always carry a flask. Have just a nip of this; it will
pull you together.'

She did not stop him from pouring the whisky into
the silver cap of the flask, and although she didn't like
the spirit, she drank it almost gratefully.

'Well, we'd better get going. That's if you want to.
I'm willing to stay longer.'

She said, 'Let me sit for a moment,' and as she made
this statement she knew she was asking for time, not
only because she felt ill but because somewhere in the
back of her mind was a fierce longing to see the woman
Paul had kept secretly from her all these years.

The sickness subsided and she sat gazing through

the trees towards the gate, with Bill Tapley by her side
quietly smoking. He knew what she was waiting for.
She was just about to say 'Let's go,' when she heard
the children's voices again. Then they came into view.
They were dancing up and down on the narrow garden
pathway, and with them was a woman. She was tall
and had a child in her arms. They were looking towards
the garage and a car being backed into the main road.
Alison now watched the woman walk slowly down
the path. She was wearing a headscarf, but even if
she hadn't been, it would have been impossible to
have seen her features plainly from this distance. She
now watched Paul getting out of the car; the children
were bouncing at his side, hanging on to each hand,
and he bent down and kissed them. It was painful
for Alison as she watched them both clinging to his
neck, but the pain was nothing compared with when
he walked to the gate, and leaning forward, kissed
the baby, then the woman. Alison did not close her
eyes. What she was watching was the departure of
a familiar figure. Paul had kissed that woman as a
man kissed a woman he had lived with for years;
not passionately on the mouth as with a mistress,
but on the side of the cheek, a familiar gesture that
a husband makes to the woman who is part of his
life, part of himself. She heard the distant revving of
his car. She saw the children and the woman waving.
Then the car moved onwards and the woman turned

and walked back up the path, the children scattering before her.

Bill Tapley's hand was on hers once more. 'Come on, let's go.' He started up the car, but when they were in the main road he said, 'You're not going straight back; you're going to have something to eat.'

'I couldn't. Thanks, but I couldn't.'

'Well, you're going to try.'

'No. No, I want to go home.'

'Sure?'

She nodded her head. 'Good enough,' he said. 'But we'll let him have some distance. I don't want to run into him at the traffic lights.'

As they neared Sealock, Bill Tapley, turning his head slightly towards her, said, 'The sale will be over. We'll call in and you can take that stuff.'

She did not reply. She had quite forgotten about . . . 'The written-in lot'. Yet but for it, she knew that she would have gone on living without the knowledge that was at this moment tearing her apart.

In the corner of the saleroom, among a few scattered people, Alison wrote out a cheque, while Bill Tapley stood beside her, much to the puzzled speculation of those about them, and when she had handed her cheque in and had given the numbered slip to a porter, he still waited by her side. Then with a twisted smile, he said, 'You won't hold today against me, will you? You know the old saying "All's fair in love and war". Anyway, I think it's about time you got yourself straightened out with regards to him. He's played on your emotions long enough.'

She was prevented from making any reply to this by the porter handing her a cardboard box in which he had stacked the plates and tea-caddy. 'Give them here.' Bill Tapley took the box from the man and, walking away, said over his shoulder, 'You can't carry this. I'll run you to the shop.'

Alison was now conscious of and embarrassed by the amused gaze of the porter who had witnessed their battle earlier in the day.

Before getting into the car she said quietly, 'I don't think that you should come to the shop.'

'Why not? All the cards will soon be on the table. And anyway, I have no intention of coming in. But you can't carry this. Get in.'

Within a few minutes they had arrived at the shop and there, right outside, was Paul's car. Bill Tapley's caustic comment of, 'He came straight back, too,' did not elicit any retort from her, but getting out and taking the box he handed to her, she looked downwards as she said, 'Thanks.'

He was standing in front of her, peering at her through the now fading light, and light rain. 'Do you mean that?'

'Yes. Yes, I do. I thank you for opening my eyes.'

'I'll be seeing you, then. And if you want any help, just give me a ring.'

She turned from him and went into the shop, to be greeted by Nelson with, 'What you got there, eh?'

She shook her head. 'Oh, a few things I bought privately for . . . for a customer.'

'Oh, let's have a look.'

'No, leave them, Nelson.' She held the box closely to her and turned her body from him. 'I'm taking them upstairs. They're going straight away again.'

'Oh!' The patch over his eye was lifted when he raised his eyebrows, but he said nothing more and she went upstairs . . . not straight to the drawing-room but into her bedroom. There she put the box into her wardrobe and took the precaution of locking the door. Then taking off her hat and coat, she looked at herself in the mirror and was amazed and dismayed at what she saw. Her face looked lifeless . . . dead. She went out of the room, up the second flight and into the drawing-room.

'Oh, almost on my tail!' Paul had turned from the mantelpiece to greet her. 'I've just got in.'

She saw at once that he was in a very good mood, quite different from that in which he had left the house and herself earlier in the day. And she knew the reason for the change . . . there was no mystery any more. Today she had had the explanation of his varying moods over the past months . . . over the past years.

It must have been difficult for him running two homes. The cold way in which this thought presented itself to her caused the deeply emotional side of her to rear and cry silently, I hate him! Oh, how I hate him!

'You look cold,' he said.

'I am cold.'

'Where have you been? What have you been doing with yourself?' He was reaching for his pipe and the easy, relaxed manner that she had loved was in evidence again. She said slowly, 'I've been to Eastbourne.'

'Oh, Eastbourne! I've just come from there myself. What where you doing in Eastbourne?'

She did not answer and her silence turned him about to look at her searchingly. She kept up the silence for a space of time and then she said flatly, 'I was watching you.' The silence was between them again. Then with his eyes wide and his lower jaw drooping, he brought out slowly, 'You . . . mean . . . you . . . followed me?'

'Yes, I followed you.'

She watched him straighten up and he seemed to swell before her eyes. Then with his teeth clenched and his lips spread he gazed at her for a moment in frightening fury before exploding: 'You blasted little . . . !' He took another breath and gritted his teeth to prevent the word escaping. With his breath slowly subsiding he said, 'Well, I hope you enjoyed what you saw and you hadn't too long to wait. But let me tell you –' he took a step towards her and so frightening was his attitude that she backed away from him. 'Let me tell you. I don't give a damn what you saw. You would get it all wrong anyway. What I object to is being spied on. You couldn't wait, could you? I told you I wanted you to come to Eastbourne with me tomorrow. But you couldn't wait.'

'Apparently I've waited long enough.'

'Oh? So you've waited long enough! What damn business is it of yours, anyway, what I do or where I go? But I'm telling you, you've got this all wrong. I know what you're thinking.'

'Yes, I'm bound to be wrong. A woman with four children, and her husband away, and you visiting at least once a week I'm bound to be wro—'

She shrank back under his uplifted hand as she waited for the blow to descend on her, and from out of the corner of her screwed-up eyes she saw the quivering fist hovering at the side of her face. She watched it tighten into a white bony mass, before it swiftly dropped away.

When at last she straightened up, he had his back to her. His head was bowed and he was supporting himself on the edge of a small table.

She too needed support. She leant against the back of a high chair. Paul had almost hit her. In her mind's eye she saw the notches on the stanchion of the door in the shop. She watched him now rubbing his hand over his eyes as if trying to obliterate the scene. The silence went on so long that she thought they would never speak again; and then his voice, rusty sounding, as if from long disuse, said, 'Why didn't you ask me about this?'

It was some time before she could say, 'How could I? Something you had kept secret for years.'

He had turned quickly to her. 'A secret? I never kept it secret. I just did not see any reason why you should be told. You were too young when it happened, and there was a definite reason why I couldn't take you to that house before. Yet tomorrow you would have known everything . . . Tomorrow . . . one more day. But as for keeping it secret, I've kept nothing secret . . . What made you follow me as if I were . . . were—' he stopped and moved slowly towards her again; and their eyes holding fast, he said sadly, 'Oh, Alison, why did you do this? Tell me.' He shook his head, 'Who put you on to this? Who suggested that I was . . . ?'

'It doesn't matter, it doesn't matter.'

'It does matter. It means a lot to me.' His hands came out and moved towards her shoulders, but she shrank away from him and he stood for a second with his arms outstretched in mid-air; then thrusting them down to his sides he barked, 'Don't do that. Don't shrink from me as if I were . . .' With a swift movement his hands came up again and he gripped her shoulders. 'Listen to me, Alison. I want to know who told you about this. Come on.' He began to shake her now as he growled, 'I won't let up until you tell me.'

Her head was bobbing on her shoulders. 'All right. All right.' She could tell him. As Bill Tapley had said, the cards were on the table, and she had no hope that any explanation of his would make Bill Tapley a liar. She pushed at him with her hands, gasping, 'Stop it. Leave go, I'll tell you.'

When they were apart once more, she had to wait until she regained her breath before, her head moving up and down, she said, 'Bill ... Bill Tapley. He ... he wanted to prove to me that ... that ...'

He broke in on her, 'Bill Tapley! Tapley? The swine!' The words were deep, slow and low. 'And he took you over there?'

Her silence was his answer.

'The car in the wood? My God!' He shook his head heavily. 'The dirty devil. And you in there with him ... Ugh!' He almost spat at her, and then he was across the room and into the hall before she could cry, 'Paul! Paul!'

Mrs Dickenson, coming out of the kitchen, said, 'What is it? He's gone past there like the devil in a gale of wind. Aren't you going to have any ... ?'

Alison almost pushed the older woman over in her headlong rush towards the stairhead door, and she leapt down the stairs after him, calling, 'Paul! Paul!' When he reached the door leading into the shop he surprised her by turning and waiting for her, and she grasped the banisters as she was pulled to a halt by the expression on his face. She had never seen Paul with an expression like this: wild, almost ferocious. And she didn't recognise his voice either when he growled, 'You stay where you are. Do you hear?'

She did not move until the door closed behind him, but when she heard the key turn in the lock she rushed at the door and battered it with her fists, again shouting, 'Paul! Paul!' She was still hammering when the door was unlocked and there stood Nelson. He looked a very perturbed old man, of which he gave evidence when he said, 'God! Miss Alison, what's got into him? Aa haven't seen him like that for years. Something's radically wrong, that's a fact.'

He had hardly finished speaking before she pushed past him and rushed through the shop, but as she pulled open the door she was only in time to see the back of Paul's car as it moved away.

Nelson was behind her, speaking to her again. 'Come in, miss, out of that. Look, you have no coat and it's pouring.'

Alison paused for a moment, then taking no heed of Nelson's voice calling after her, she ran down the hill, straight through Badger's Alleyway, across the square, skirting the wall by the old disused cemetery, then through short cuts and side streets until she arrived at the end of the Regency terrace. Through the driving rain and the dimmed street lights she saw Paul's car drawn up by the kerb, and as she raced up the street towards it, past the curious glances of the rain-protected passers-by, her heart was pounding as if it would burst from her body.

The green door was ajar, the hall was lit, and although there was no-one to be seen the whole house seemed to be reverberating with voices. She made for the drawing-room, and there they were in the centre of the room facing each other, and her cry of ·'Paul! Paul!' was lost in the shouting.

'You've been planning this for years, you dirty swine!'

'Dirty swine, am I? Look who's talking. And who do you think you're trying to kid? You won't kid her with that tale. She might be young but she's not to be fooled with you and your side-shoot . . .'

It happened so swiftly, even in the space of her taking a step. Paul's fist shot out and Bill Tapley reeled back, staggering against a beautiful inlaid card table that went crashing over on to the stone hearth. She was hanging on to Paul now, crying, 'Stop it! . . . Don't! Don't! Paul, listen to me.'

But he was not listening, he was watching with furious gaze and unblinking eyes as Bill Tapley rose slowly to his feet. He watched him grope out behind him and grip the back of a chair, then stand shaking his head and slowly moving his fingers over his bleeding mouth and along the line of his jaw before bringing his hand from his face. And now, looking from his blood-stained palm towards Paul, he muttered slowly, 'You shouldn't have done that. Talking's one thing, this is another.' His fingers were touching his jaw again. 'You'll be sorry for this. If I have to wait a lifetime, I'll make you sorry for this, Paul Aylmer.'

Alison clung on tightly to Paul as she felt the muscles of his arms contracting again, and as she looked at Bill Tapley there was no feeling of sympathy in her, for here was the real Bill Tapley again, cunning, wary, waiting; not the man he had presented to her this afternoon. He was looking at her now, speaking to her through closed teeth. 'Don't be hoodwinked by any soft-soap tale he'll tell you . . . You saw for yourself this afternoon.'

Paul's whole body jerked as if about to spring again, but he did not move forward. He remained still and silent for a moment before saying thickly, 'You always were a snake, Tapley. I've been wary of you for years. I knew what you were working up to and I've played you at your own game. If she hadn't hated your guts I would have stepped in before, but I knew that any move you made would be turned down flat, so I let you go on. But you couldn't wait to play your cards; and you pushed them too far today. You should have been more patient and gone on with your plan, which was to marry her, get her money out of the firm and break me . . . once again. That was it, wasn't it?'

'I'll do it yet.' Bill Tapley was carefully wiping the blood from his face with a handkerchief.

At this point Alison realised that neither man was aware of her presence; they were taken up in this moment with their hate of each other. This hate that had materialised long before she had come on to the scene. Yet it was she who had brought it to a head.

At this point Paul shrugged off Alison's hold, and his lip curled upwards, leaving his large teeth bare as he muttered deep in his throat, 'I'll be ready for you. And when you try it, I'll give you the same treatment I would a snake. It's a good job I knew your father or I would have been deceived by your smarm more than once, but there's not a pin to put between you. He'll be alive until you're dead. He once said to me there were different ways of crucifying a man, and by God! you've learned well from him. But I'm warning you, Tapley, you step near my preserves again' – at this point he actually pushed Alison before him – 'you won't get off as lightly as you did this time. Remember you can drive a man so far that he comes to a point where he doesn't give a damn. I've reached that point, so just remember that.'

When Alison once again found herself pushed, and roughly, towards the door she did not protest. And as they went out of the house, no word of retaliation from Bill Tapley followed them.

As she stepped into the street Paul pulled the car door open and almost thrust her inside. Then going round into his seat, he started the engine and let in the clutch so quickly that the car seemed to leap from the road.

She was shivering again, but now partly from cold. She was wet through and suddenly very tired, as if she herself had been doing battle, and she wanted desperately to bend her head and cry.

It was a matter of minutes later that she realised they were not on the road leading to the house. They were on the main road with the traffic skimming past like phantoms through the rain. Turning to him, she brought out quickly, 'Where ... where are we going?' When he did not answer she cried, 'Paul, look! Where are we going? What are you doing?'

His voice was cold and impersonal as he answered, 'We are going to Eastbourne. You like Eastbourne, so we're going back there.'

Her shivering became intensified, and now she felt frightened. She said quickly, 'I don't want to go. I want to go home; I'm tired.'

'That's your lookout; you should have thought about that in the first place.'

She peered at his steely profile through the dim light. This wasn't Paul, this was a stranger. And she tried to keep the tremor out of her voice when she said, 'I don't want to go to Eastbourne. I want to hear nothing more.'

'It has ceased to matter to me what you want. But I want you to go to Eastbourne, and that's where you're going. After that you can go where you like.'

'Paul!' Her voice was a whimper now, but he took no heed of the pain in it.

After turning a corner at a speed that made her gasp he muttered thickly, as if to himself, 'Sitting in the wood! peeping . . . prying . . . My God!'

'Oh, Paul, it was the shock . . . finding out like that.'

'Finding out what, like that?' The car was filled with his voice now. 'You took his word that everything he said about me was true. Why couldn't you wait and ask me? Anything but trail me and spy on me. And what is more, if I were keeping ten women, it's no business of either yours or his.' His head came round to her and his eyes blazed in her direction, and so long did he look at her that she became alarmed for the safety of them both. She bowed her head. He was right, she should never have listened to Bill Tapley. She should have waited until Paul came in and asked him to explain everything. Even now she couldn't see how he could explain the situation away. Yet some part of her was fearing – and that was the word, fearing – that Bill Tapley had been wrong.

By the time the car stopped she was shivering all

over and she had to press her teeth together to try to stop them chattering. He opened the car door for her, then again he pushed her, now towards the garden gate. But once she was on the path he went ahead of her to the front door.

Alison's head was drooped when the door opened. She could only see the feet and skirt of a woman standing in a dim light. But when the woman said, 'Why, Paul, what brings you back? What's the matter?' she raised her head.

It was a lovely voice she heard, cultured and sweet. And then she was looking at the woman's face, at her startled eyes and the hand moving up to protect the cheek; but she had seen all there was to see before the woman moved aside, saying, 'Do come in. Come in.'

Alison moved slowly into the little hall. Already she was bowed down with shame. Whatever she was to learn about Paul now didn't seem to matter. If he told her pointedly that he loved this woman, she could understand it. He had always been compassionate and kind, and this woman needed compassion and kindness, for one side of her face was seared and scarred in such a fashion that the sight of it made you want to look away.

She had told herself not to turn her eyes away, but to keep looking at the woman as if the face was that of an ordinary woman. But she hadn't been able to do this.

'Margaret, this is Alison. I brought her over so that I could explain things.' His voice was slightly calmer now and the woman, after looking at him intently, said in a quiet tone, 'But I thought it was to be tomorrow, Paul.'

'Yes, it was to have been tomorrow.' Although Alison's head was bent she knew that Paul was looking at her. 'But something happened this afternoon that precipitated matters.'

No-one spoke for a moment, then the woman was standing before Alison, her hand on the sleeve of her dress, and she said in surprised tones, 'But you're wet.' Then turning her head towards Paul she added, 'She's wet through, Paul.'

This statement elicited no sympathetic reply and into the embarrassing silence the woman spoke again: 'You must get those wet things off, my dear. Come along into my room.'

'I'm all right.'

'Do as you're told.' It was Paul speaking, as if to an errant, disobedient child. It was more than she could take, and she turned towards him sharply, saying, 'Don't speak to me like that; I've had enough. If I'm wrong, I'm wrong. But don't speak to me like that.'

'Uncle! Is that Uncle? Is that Uncle Paul?' Children's voices came from a bedroom at the end of the hall and the woman called, 'Be quiet! and stay where you are. He'll be with you in a minute.' On this she again put her hand on Alison's arm, and turning her about, led her into a bedroom, saying, 'I've just got them bathed and into bed.' When the door was closed, she went to the wardrobe and took out a dress and a dressing-gown. 'These will be much too big for you,' she said, 'but they'll be dry.'

Alison was standing helplessly before the woman on the good side of her face, and even then there was no sign of beauty. But she had something, some quality. The way she held herself. Her quiet manner. Above all, her voice. All the beauty she needed was in her voice. The woman handed her a towel now, saying, 'Dry your hair, it's dripping, you don't want to catch cold.' Then she said suddenly, 'You're exactly as Paul described you to me.'

The towel in her hand, Alison stared at the woman, who went on, 'He's wanted to bring you for such a long time, but I wouldn't have it. You see' – she turned to the dressing-table which, Alison was quick to note, was without a mirror – 'Well, I'm rather shy of people. You can understand that.' Her head was lowered. 'I knew from his description that you were beautiful. I thought that you, being young, I . . . I might frighten you. I . . . I have seen a young girl turn away from me before today, so . . . so I don't often go out, or see anyone. I don't want to see people, but when Paul brought the necklace over, he said that things must be explained to you.'

'The necklace? Mrs Gordon-Platt's necklace?' Alison was about to put her arms into the dressing-gown, but stopped.

'Mrs Gordon-Platt is my mother. I was Margaret Gordon-Platt.'

'Margaret Gordon-Platt?' Alison whispered the words.

'Yes, Margaret Gordon-Platt. It's a long story. Come along, put the dressing-gown on and we'll have a cup of tea.'

It was an absolutely mystified Alison whom Margaret led from the room. As they reached the hall the children's voices assailed them, shouting in chorus, 'Uncle Paul! Uncle Paul! Why aren't you coming in, Uncle Paul?'

'If you don't stop making that noise I won't let him come in at all. He's going to have a cup of tea, so be quiet.'

'Oh, Mummy, let him come in. Please. Please.'

The voices trailed off and there was a sound of scuffling and giggling, and as Alison listened, a separate pain entered into her. There was something about the atmosphere in this little house that spelt home.

When she entered the sitting-room the feeling was emphasised by Paul standing with his back to the fire, for he too looked at home and a little less angry than he had done.

'There, sit yourself down until I make a cup of tea.'

Margaret was ushering Alison to a chair when Paul said, 'I've put the kettle on; it'll be some minutes. You sit down, Margaret.'

After Margaret had seated herself at one end of the small couch, Paul took his seat beside her, sitting quite close. In this position he faced Alison and his eyes held hers for a moment before lifting Margaret's hand and holding it tenderly. 'This is my cousin Robert's wife,' he said. 'She used to be Margaret Gordon-Platt . . .'

Margaret interrupted him gently at this point, saying, 'She knows that, Paul.'

'Well, what I'm sure she doesn't know is that the children in the next room aren't mine, although I wish they were.' His eyes were holding Alison's.

'Oh, Paul!' Margaret pulled her hand from his and slapped him sharply as she said, 'You don't need to say things like that, for you don't mean them.'

'I do. It's the truth, and she's got to know the truth. But she's heard so many lies already – and believed them – that I doubt whether she'll recognise the truth when she hears it. Anyway, I'll go back and start at the beginning . . . Right?' He nodded his head at Alison as if expecting some comment, but when she just continued to stare at him he went on, 'My uncle, Leonard Welsh, was head gardener to Mrs Gordon-Platt in the old days. He had a son, Robert. And Margaret here . . . and Robert . . . well, you could almost say they grew up side by side . . .'

Alison found that she was listening to Paul's voice yet not taking in his words. There seemed to be no need, for she knew the story and she was in this moment overwhelmed with shame. She should have known, oh, she should have known, after living with Paul for eight years, that he wouldn't live the underhand life of which she had accused him. Was it any wonder that he was burned up with anger against her?

Her attention was brought back to Paul as he said, 'Time and again Margaret tried to make it up with her mother, but to no avail. The price of being taken back into the family fold was that she should leave her husband. Then at just about this time, you came on to my horizon and Robert took ill with TB. He has been in and out of hospital ever since . . . There now . . . are you satisfied? Does this explain my double life?'

She lowered her head further for a moment then in self-defence she jerked it upwards, saying, 'I wasn't an idiot, you know, someone you couldn't have talked to. You could have explained, some of it, anyway . . .'

'I'm afraid that's my fault.' Margaret was leaning towards her now. 'He wanted to bring you here a long time ago but I wouldn't let him, and he thought it would only complicate things if he told you of the situation, yet continued to visit without you. He thought you wouldn't understand a woman who couldn't bear the sight of other women, beautiful women . . . I'm better now, because I've learned to live with myself, but there was a time when I couldn't. You mustn't blame Paul for this; if there's anyone to blame, it's me. You see . . .' Margaret swallowed and began to pick agitatedly at the first finger of her left hand, only to have Paul put in quietly, 'You go and make the tea, Margaret, and I'll finish the explaining. Go on now.' He patted her arm, then pushed her gently, and she rose swiftly from the sofa and went out of the room.

Now they were alone, Alison found that she couldn't meet Paul's eyes. All she desired in this moment was to throw herself on him and beg his forgiveness. But, from the look on his face, she knew that this wasn't the moment, and she doubted if there would ever be a moment when he would allow her even to come near him again, really near . . . close. He was talking now, his voice low and rapid. 'Just after Angela, the first baby, was born, Margaret was knocked down by a bus. She was so badly injured they doubted if she would live. The injuries to her face meant a long, long period of plastic surgery, operation after operation. She came home for a short while before she was due to go to the hospital at East Grinstead. It was during this period that she realised Robert was sick. They hadn't long taken this smallholding and everything had gone wrong. Robert was trying to look after the baby and run the place – he didn't bother about himself – with the result he collapsed three days before Margaret was to go into hospital again. So instead of her going, it was Robert who went, and he was there for nearly a year. If it hadn't been for the child, Margaret would have gone ahead with the operations, but she refused to leave Angela in anyone's care. Robert doted on the child and it worried him to think of it being put out to nurse. He had no relative alive except myself. So there you have it. The pattern that has been repeated over the years. Robert would be all right for a short time, then back again to hospital. Margaret had a second baby and then a third, and a fourth, because she wants them, they are her life . . . a reason for living. She has worked like a trojan to keep things going here and all to no avail . . . And that is why, when I saw that part of the necklace, I wanted to bring it to her and let her decide what was to be done with it, for it's hers by right. Let me tell you, I don't believe for a moment that the old woman meant her to have it, because when she knew that Margaret had had a bad accident she didn't even write to her and was heard to remark that there was a saying about making beds and lying on them, and that her offer still stood.'

Alison hated to think that Mrs Gordon-Platt was the type of woman Paul was describing, yet she had to believe him.

Paul was speaking again, 'Everything's mortgaged up to the hilt here – those stones would be a godsend.

The bank manager would be very pleased to see them, I know that . . .'

'Why didn't you help them?' The question was out before she could stop it.

'For the simple reason,' he said slowly, 'that I'd used up your money – Tapley told me he had told you about that – and I did use it, I make no bones about it. Old Tapley was charging me six per cent on the loan he made me and it was throttling me. I could see myself slowly drowning as the years went on . . . working . . . working to pay that interest. Then you, like a gift from the gods, put into my hands eighteen thousand pounds. Without any compunction whatever I used it, knowing that, given a fair deal, I could put back every penny, and I've almost done that. The careful investments I made in . . . war stock and such have nearly replaced the capital. The interest, I'm afraid, will have to wait a little while longer. But don't worry, you'll get it, and the sooner the better, for then I'll be clear of the whole damned burden. Anyway, there you have your answer. That is why I haven't been able to help Robert and Margaret . . . At least, not in a way that would make much impression upon the difficulties they are in now.'

'Oh, Paul, please.' She saw he was staring at her as if he hated the sight of her. 'Please' – she was pleading with him – 'take the money; I don't want it. Please.'

'Even if I wanted to marry Freda Gordon-Platt?'

If he had lifted his fist and struck her in the face

she could not have felt more shattered. In spite of his manner and anger against her, he had almost been her Paul again, and now he had said, 'Even if I wanted to marry Freda Gordon-Platt.' She wished she was big enough, not in body, but in spirit and in heart to be the kind of person who loved him in such a way that she could say, Yes, even if you want to marry her, take what you want. But she wasn't that kind of person. The very thought of Mrs Freda Gordon-Platt touching anything that belonged to her was enough to send anger flaming through her.

He was waiting for her answer and she gave it to him. 'I wouldn't want Mrs Freda Gordon-Platt to have a farthing of mine, so there.'

'Even if you knew that she too had suffered and was up against it?'

'Even if I knew that; I'm no hypocrite. I don't like the woman and never have since the first moment I saw her.'

'But you haven't the same feeling towards her son?'

She moved her head slowly. Here they were, off again on the wrong tack; but if he could hurt, so could she and she replied, 'No, I haven't. I don't know how he comes to be her son. He's too nice to have any connection with her whatever.'

'I'm sure he's very happy to know how you feel.'

At this point Margaret entered the room carrying

the tea-tray and Paul turned hurriedly to take it from her.

'There now.' Margaret sat down with the unscarred side of her face towards Alison, but when she turned to hand her the cup the terrible destruction of tissue was in full view. Alison's heart once again went out to this woman, and she remembered something that Nelson had once said about his losing the sight of his right eye. 'Aa've had plenty of time to weigh the whole thing up,' he had said, 'and my feeling about it now is that life isn't complete unless you're given a cross to carry.' Well, age might have brought philosophy to Nelson's way of looking at life but it would take a lot of philosophy, she thought, to welcome the cross that this poor woman was carrying. And yet there was about her a quietness, a peace. Yes, there was a sense of peace in her presence.

Alison drank the tea gratefully, and she was handing her cup to Margaret to be refilled when the voices of the children were heard again, so Paul, laying down his cup, rose from the chair and went out of the room.

Margaret, passing the cup to Alison, now said quietly, 'Don't look so perturbed. Paul will get over his anger, and I don't blame you for thinking as you did. Not knowing the facts it was a natural conclusion. And it was my fault . . . If I had the money I would buy an island.'

'Oh, please, please don't say that. I've been a dreadful fool . . . at least where you're concerned . . .' She wasn't being a fool over Mrs Gordon-Platt, she knew that. She leant forward now towards Margaret and whispered, 'About the necklace. I'm quite agreeable that you should keep it. As Paul says, it's yours by right.'

'Yes, I know.' Margaret nodded her head slowly. 'But as I told Paul in the beginning, I would rather go to my mother and see what she has to say about it. But Paul is all against that.'

Alison could understand why Paul was against such a move. Freda Gordon-Platt would not like the idea of him allowing anything of value to be directed to sources other than her own. If there was anything of value to be turned into money she would consider herself, and her son, had prior claim to it.

Margaret was speaking again. Quietly she said, 'I've tried for years to mend the breach between myself and my mother, but she was always so bitter. I cannot really believe that she wants to see me now.'

'But she does,' Alison put in quickly. 'Beck says that she kept the necklace particularly for you and hid it so that no-one else would get their hands on it.'

'She's a strange woman. She always was. We never understood each other. Charles was her whole life and when he left her and went abroad she became embittered . . . suspicious.' She turned her face fully to Alison now and asked abruptly, 'Do you like Mrs Freda?'

'No, I don't.'

'Nor do I.' A faint smile spread across the contorted features. 'I never have done, and now she's trying to get back on the old footing with Paul and she'll only bring him misery. I know she will. She did years ago. And he deserves so much. I just dare not think what would have happened to us as a family if it hadn't been for Paul. He has helped Robert again and again and kept us afloat. When he himself was sinking he kept us afloat. He's a wonderful person, is Paul.' She paused here, looking steadily at Alison, then added, 'He's greatly attached to you. You've made such a difference to his life.'

'I might have done at one time, but I don't now. He has his own life, apparently.' Alison was staring at her twisting fingers.

'I don't believe that, not really. He loves you—'

'Did he say that?' Alison interrupted, turning to look at Margaret again.

'He has no need to say it. He's not a man who talks about himself or his feelings. You judge him mostly by his actions. But one would have to be stupid not to realise that he loves you.'

But had he always loved her? Yes, she could believe that. As a child he had loved her and as a girl he had loved her. But that was not the way she wanted to be loved. She wanted to be loved in the same way he loved Freda Gordon-Platt, in a way that would make him take a sword in his hand and make great marks in an oak stanchion.

Margaret said abruptly now, 'I haven't seen my nephew, Roy, but I understand he is a very presentable young man ... You have seen him a number of times?'

'Yes. Well, not so often; three or four times.'

'You like him?'

Alison's lids wavered, then drooped before she answered, 'Yes. Yes, I like him. He's a very nice boy, and I can say, and not for the first time, that he is very different from his mother.'

'Thinking that way, it's going to be very awkward for you if you get to more than like him, isn't it?'

Alison's eyes widened just the slightest, and she repeated, 'More than like him? ... But ...' She paused as Paul came back into the room. He was buttoning his coat and speaking to Margaret the while: 'The dress is almost dry; I've taken it off the boiler, Margaret. I think we'll be getting back.'

'Oh, all right, Paul.' Margaret smiled and stood up; and then turning to Alison, said, 'Would you like to come along? That is, if you're ready.'

'Yes, I'm ready.' Alison cast a look in Paul's direction that wasn't pleasant. He hadn't asked *her* whether she was ready or not. Although she was very sorry for what she had done this afternoon, she resented being treated like a recalcitrant child, especially in front of someone else, and someone as nice as this woman.

As she passed him, Paul returned her look, and it was no more pleasant than her own.

A few minutes later, wearing an old mackintosh of Margaret's, she took her leave, promising to come back when she could to see the children. She hadn't, she noted, been asked to go into the bedroom to see them, and in a way this added to the feeling of being one apart . . . shut out from Paul and his interests.

They never spoke one word to each other during the whole journey home, as though they were waiting, Alison thought, until they got indoors, when the sparks would fly once more. Oh, she was tired. She had begun to shiver again and felt a little sick. This decided her that no matter how he might provoke her with his temper and arrogance, she would have no further words with him that night. She would not even go with him into the drawing-room. She would go straight to her room and to bed. The last thought brought a glow of comfort – all she wanted to do was to get into bed and be warm.

But when the car drew up outside the shop, there with his finger on the bell stood Roy Gordon-Platt.

'Oh! hello,' he called, and in the headlights his pleasure was plainly evident. 'I'd almost given up; I thought you were out.' He laughed, 'And of course you were.' He was now speaking through the open window to Alison. Paul still sat in the driving seat and it seemed that he had no intention of getting out of the car. Then he thrust the car door open and stalked to the shop door. He did not speak to Roy, not even to acknowledge his presence, and it would have been plain to anyone but a boy very much in love that he was not wanted. But at this moment Roy was apparently blind or indifferent to Paul's cursory treatment, for he kept on talking to Alison, almost chattering to her. 'I phoned twice this afternoon and my mother was down this way and she called, too. And at tea-time she said, why didn't I pop over and see if you are still alive, so here I am,' he finished on a laugh.

In the darkness of the shop doorway Alison didn't need to look at him. If she had been forced to, she would have had to close her eyes against his youth. He was so juvenile, so much younger than his years . . . So his mother had been over this afternoon, had she? She was definitely keeping the place warm. They were in the dark shop now and Paul had strode away without switching on the door light. As she pressed the switch, Alison thought angrily, he's going to be more awkward and beastly than ever now. It really was so unjust. If *he* could keep company with the mother, why couldn't *she* keep company with the son if she wanted to? She wished at this moment, from the bottom of her heart, that she wanted to keep company with the son. It would have solved her problem.

Over her shoulder she said to Roy, 'Be careful of this table, there are vases on it.' She held out her hand as a guide and was not amused when it was grabbed and held on to. She steered him past the table but he did not relinquish his hold and, hand in hand, they reached the staircase door. Alison was thinking, what does it matter, when Paul's voice came from out of the dimness, startling her as he said, 'Well, what are we waiting for?'

She had imagined that he had already gone upstairs. She snatched her hand away from Roy's and raced up the two flights of stairs.

In the softly lit drawing-room the fire was blazing, the meal was set at the dining-room end, and everything was shining and inviting. It could have been so wonderful. It *had* been wonderful this time last week.

'This is a beautiful room.' As Roy stood looking about him, Alison walked towards the fire without making any comment, and it suddenly seemed to dawn on the boy that the atmosphere was strained. Alison was now crouching down on the rug, her hands held out to the blaze, but then Roy's voice came to her saying, 'I had better be going, for I had no intention of staying. I just came to ask you, sir' – he was now addressing Paul – 'if you would phone Mother around eight o'clock.' At this Alison turned her head towards Roy. She felt full of contrition that he should have been made to feel unwelcome. But now her eyes turned to Paul, for he had swung round from the sideboard and was staring at the boy in an odd way.

'She would have come with me,' Roy went on, 'but she's not feeling too good. She's had a headache all day. Well, I'll be off. Goodbye, Alison. I'll . . . I'll phone you, if I may.'

'Yes. Yes, do that, Roy. I'm sorry . . .' Then her voice trailed off as Paul said brusquely, 'I'll see you out,' adding, 'Would you care for a drink before you go?'

'No. No, thank you, sir. Goodbye, Alison.' He turned towards Alison again, his expression naked.

Alison watched him leave, Paul following, and when she had the room to herself she slumped down on the rug feeling exhausted. But a few minutes later, when she heard Paul mounting the stairs again, she rose shakily to her feet. She must go to bed. She couldn't do any more battle with him tonight. She felt too awful.

As Paul entered the room at the dining-room end, she left by the drawing-room door, going straight down to her room, where she switched on the electric blanket and after quickly undressing, got into bed. While she waited for the blanket to warm up she lay shivering. But even when it was giving off a good heat she still shivered.

She had been in bed for three-quarters of an hour when she heard two sharp raps on the door. She did not answer, because if she unclenched her teeth they would start to chatter again. A few seconds later the door opened and Paul was standing over her and pulling back the bedclothes from her face. Bending quickly down to her, his voice was a little less abrupt but still not Paul's voice, 'Are you cold?' he asked.

'Y . . . yes. I'm freezing.'

He put his hand on her head, then felt her wrist, after which he remarked casually, 'Your pulse seems to be normal.' And on this he turned and walked quickly out of the room.

Five minutes later he was back again standing over her. 'Come on,' he said, 'Get up; I've run a mustard bath. Soak in that and then I'll give you some hot whisky. It'll ward it off.'

'I don't want to get up. I'm so cold.'

'You won't be so cold if you get into the bath. Get up and don't be silly.'

Oh, if only he wouldn't speak to her like that. She pulled herself up into a sitting position, saying, 'All right, leave me alone.'

It was with an effort that she got out of bed and put on her dressing-gown and went upstairs. The bathroom was steaming and hot, and when she lowered herself into the water she murmured thankfully, 'Oh, beautiful, beautiful.' And after a few minutes of soaking she thought it would be very pleasant to die like this.

Twenty minutes later she was back in bed and choking over a glass of hot whisky. 'I . . . I can't drink any more.'

'Drink it up, every drop of it.'

'But . . . but you know I don't like hot whisky.'

'There are lots of things we don't like but have got to do . . . Drink it up.'

She moved her head impatiently, closed her eyes and with an effort emptied the glass. Then, shuddering violently from the effects of the whisky, she lay down, turning her face away from him. The next moment she heard him switch off the light, leaving only a wall-light on in the far corner of the room. And then the door closed and she was alone, with a mountain of self-pity for company.

When he had had the flu she had looked after him . . . nursed him at all hours. Whatever he had done, she would have forgiven him if only because he felt ill, she knew she would. He was hard, unforgiving, and unjust. So unjust. So ran her thoughts until, the whisky taking effect, she slowly dropped into sleep.

She must have slept for a long while before waking, her body running with perspiration and her hair clammy. After this she dropped into fitful dozes, awakening briefly to find herself talking. At one point she awoke shouting out aloud and flinging her arms about. Her arm struck against something, and she felt her hand taken gently and pressed down under the clothes. As her hair was lifted from her sweating brow and neck, she kept her eyes closed. Paul was with her. He was sitting as he used to do when she had toothache or laryngitis. Paul was nice, Paul was wonderful. The fingers moving on her brow wiped away any thoughts of a Mrs Freda Gordon-Platt. There was only Paul and her in the whole world. The past week had been but a feverish dream. Yes, she had dreamt it all. There was no Bill Tapley and a car parked in a wood. Paul would never have taken her by the shoulders and shaken her violently; Paul would never shout at her. Paul was wonderful, Paul was good. She put out her hand and caught at the fingers, and holding them fast, she dropped off to sleep again.

The next time Alison woke Paul was still there, this time with a cup of tea. He said quietly, 'How do you feel now?'

How did she feel? She closed her eyes again for a second. She felt sapped and tired but the shivery feeling had gone. She said, 'I feel better.'

He said, 'You should stay where you are today.'

She did not protest, since the last thing she felt like doing was getting up. He stood beside the bed as she drank the tea, and when she handed back the cup their eyes met for a flashing second. The gulf between them was still there but filled now with embarrassment. He was no longer angry, as he had been yesterday. He was once more his quiet, reserved self. He could even be tender to her, although the gulf would remain. He said now, 'Can you eat anything? Some toast?'

She shook her head. 'No, thanks.'

'Another cup of tea, perhaps?' As he made to turn from the bed he paused, saying, 'As soon as Nellie is here, I'll have to go. I've made arrangements to view some pieces in Balfour Terrace. Then I've an appointment at twelve. I won't be in for lunch, but I should be back just after two.'

Alone once more, Alison lay gazing up at the ceiling. He had an appointment for lunch. Well, what did it matter? He would do what he wanted; he was made that way. He wanted to pick up the threads of the past and he was grasping them with both hands. But she felt so low, so awful, that she couldn't even think up a caustic comment to make about Freda Gordon-Platt.

When he brought her a second cup of tea he handed her two pills, saying, 'Take these.'

'What are they?'

'They're the ones the doctor gave me.'

She held them on the palm of her hand and said, 'Oh, but they'll make me sleepy. No, I don't want them.'

'Take them. Go on, take them.'

She put the pills on her tongue and drank some tea.

As she laid the cup on the bedside table she noticed he did not go but stood looking at her for so long that she felt he was about to say something, something important. She glanced up at him, at the face of the Paul she loved, and waited, her eyes on his and held fast now. She watched his lips move twice as he prepared to speak, and then abruptly he turned about and was gone.

Well, what would he have said if he had spoken? Would he have tried to enlist her sympathy for Mrs Gordon-Platt? She was always irritated with situations in books where the hero or the heroine could have straightened out their particular muddle with a few plain words, but refrained from doing so. When she came to a part like that she generally put the book down; it was too silly. Now she asked herself if she really wanted Paul to talk. Did she . . . did she want plain speaking? No. Like the heroine in the novels, she wanted to avoid the truth. The foibles that you laughed at in others weren't amusing when they came to the fore in yourself.

She did not hear Mrs Dickenson come in, nor Paul leave the house, for she went to sleep almost immediately. She must have slept until about twelve o'clock when, dreamily, she heard Nelson saying softly, 'Aa'll just put me head round the door.' When she heard the door open she kept her eyes closed and made no movement. She did not want to talk to Nelson. The door closed again and she dozed once more. Then it was Mrs Dickenson saying, 'Come on, miss. I think you've had enough sleep for one day. Come on, sit up and get this ... How are you feeling?' Alison pulled herself up in the bed, and lying back against the bed-head, said sleepily, 'Oh, I think I'm feeling a lot better, Nellie, but I don't want anything to eat.'

'You try; just make an effort. Get through some of it. I haven't brought much. There now.' She settled the bed-table over Alison's knees, then said, 'Straight after I get me dinner I'm going to slip down to the shops. It's the best time; they're clear about now. And I'm going to call in on that butcher and give him a piece of me tongue ... Even then it'll be more tender than the steak he sent this morning.' She gave a 'hic' of a laugh. 'You could sole your boots with it. They put you off with anything when they deliver the stuff. I've always told you that, haven't I? There now.' She pushed at Alison's pillows. 'You're all settled, so enjoy that.'

To her own surprise Alison ate most of the lunch. A short time later Mrs Dickenson returned wearing her coat and hat and ready for the street, and exclaimed in a rush, 'Oh! that's good. You'll not suffer much if you can eat. Feed a cold and starve a fever; that's what they say and it's true. Well, I'm off now and

I won't be long. You'll be all right?' Alison said, 'Yes, oh, yes, I'll be all right, Nellie. I even feel like getting up.'

'Do no such thing, stay where you are. Mr Paul will be in just after two, he said. Well, here I go. Stay where you are now. Goodbye.'

'Goodbye, Nellie.'

It must have been about five minutes later that Alison heard the heavy tread on the stairs. She knew Nelson's step, and when the tap came on the door she said, 'Come in, Nelson.'

The old man shuffled across the room towards her, saying, 'How you feelin' now, eh?'

'Oh, I'm all right, Nelson. It's just a bit of a chill. I got wet last night.'

'Aa would say you would, goin' out without a coat. But Aa'll tell you what Aa've come up about, for there's something up here Aa can't understand.' He shook his head. 'Aa had it in me mind that Mr Paul had gone out to have a meal with that one the day. But there she is down in the street.' He leant over her now, whispering, 'She came and asked to see him. Aa told her he was out and she said she would wait. But Aa wouldn't let her up. Aa said you had the flu and were in a bad way. She looked at me as if she could've killed me.' He nodded his head. 'And then she stalked out of the shop. But there she is down there in the street, pretending to be looking in the windows.'

'Did you tell her what time he was coming back?'

'Aye, Aa did.' Nelson moved his head in disgust at himself. 'It slipped out. Just on two, Aa said he'd be back. That's when she said she would wait. Aa must've been daft. But Aa was taken off me guard, you know, miss, because Aa was sure he was with her. There's something funny about this business.'

'Yes, Nelson, yes. But look' – Alison was sitting up – 'get back to the shop, you never know who might come in.'

'Aye, Aa will. But you stay tucked up there.' He nodded at her and Alison nodded back at him. But once the door had closed she pushed the bedclothes aside and got out of bed. She had no doubt but that when Paul came in, Freda Gordon-Platt would be with him. And she couldn't bear to be stuck down here, she just couldn't. She needn't dress; she could just wear her dressing-gown. She could tuck up on the couch as if she had been there for some time.

To her surprise she found that her legs were unsteady, and when she looked at herself in the mirror she screwed up her nose against the reflection. She must have a wash and put on some make-up to cover up the dullness of her skin.

As she mounted the stairs to the top floor she had to hang on to the banister. It must be the effect of the pills, she told herself as she went into the bathroom. What she would like to do was have a bath to waken her up, but there mightn't be time. It was almost two o'clock and Paul could return at any moment.

She ran the taps and was actually in the process of sluicing her face when she heard the stair doorway open, then close again. Grabbing a towel, she hastily dried herself, but then realised it was too late to get into the drawing-room before they did. She could have done it if she had dropped everything and run, but she felt in no condition to run and she must put on some make-up before she came face-to-face with that madam.

She sat down on the bathroom stool and heard footsteps crossing the hall and into the drawing-room; but it did strike her as odd that she was hearing neither Paul's nor Freda Gordon-Platt's voice.

When Paul's voice did come to her, his words intrigued her. Under ordinary circumstances she would not have been able to hear what he was saying, but his voice was raised and although it was muffled she heard him say plainly, 'I don't believe you.'

Alison rose slowly from the stool. There was something in Paul's voice that was not at all lover-like. It drew her towards the bathroom door and softly she turned the handle and, without any compunction, stood there listening.

'Why should he lie?' It was Mrs Freda Gordon-Platt speaking now.

'There are a number of reasons why Tapley should lie, the main one being that he hates me.'

'But this does not concern you, it concerns her. I've just told you he said that he outbid her for the lot, then sold it back to her. And I can tell you he's as angry as I am, if not more so, and he called her some names when he knew the truth.'

'How do you know it's the truth?' Paul's voice was sharp.

'Because I know my mother-in-law. She wouldn't have gone off her head as she has done over a tea-caddy had it not been more than just a tea-caddy. And I've told you she said nothing about the stones; it was Beck who gave that away. She said that your precious ward had promised to get them back for her and was going round the salerooms to discover where they were. And do you think she would have bid up to fifty-five pounds for a few plates and a little caddy unless she knew what she was after? I could sue her for this.'

'You could do nothing of the sort.' Paul's voice was low now. 'If she's got these things . . . and I don't believe she has, but if she has, she's come by them legally. And don't forget you said she didn't get the lot – Bill Tapley got it, then sold it back to her. So everything is quite above board, as far as I can see. But she would never have done this without telling me, I know that.'

Alison put her hand tightly across her mouth and lowered her head.

'No, of course she wouldn't.' Mrs Freda Gordon-Platt's voice came sneeringly across the hall. 'You think the sun shines round her; you're besotted with her. Oh, it makes me sick, you . . . you, who are old enough to be her father.'

A silence fell upon the house now, and Alison, her head up, her heart racing, waited for Paul's answer. Then it came, revealing nothing.

'I'm not discussing Alison with you.'

'No . . . because you're afraid; afraid to face the fact that you're competing against youth. You're competing against my son . . . You know, Paul, I could feel sorry for you, because they're in love with each other. It happened like that.' There came a sound of snapping fingers; then the voice went on, 'I saw it from the beginning and I can tell you that I helped it along. I left my compact here, not planning to return for it myself, but to give Roy the chance to meet her again . . .'

And leave the field and Paul open for herself, thought Alison.

'That was very clever of you, Freda.' Paul's voice was cold. 'You always did have your eye on the main chance. When you came back on to my horizon you had everything planned, didn't you? Beacon Ride was a millstone. Like yourself, it wasn't attractive to anyone in the county. Oh, don't rear up, Freda; I know more than you think. For the past year you have tried to fling your cap where the money lies. When that didn't work, I was the last resort. I had a good business; at least, you thought so. I was the last port in your stormy life, as I had been the first. You thought you could pick up the threads where you had dropped them years ago. You made a bid for money then, and it failed. Well, you made a wrong bid again this time, Freda. That day you returned, you did me a good turn. I'd been bitter for years, bitter against life and against women, and trusting no-one. When I saw you again you seemed to lift a mountain from me. I knew I was free of you and all you had done . . . I was no longer weighed down by hate and resentment. You and your precious Charles crippled me. I could have gone to jail; I nearly did, and it rankled for years. Then, when all your other plans failed, you had the nerve to come back and think I'd be fool enough to take up the threads again. You're not really clever, you know, Freda . . .'

At this point, another voice came to Alison. It was Nelson's, calling from the bottom of the stairs: 'Mr Paul! Mr Paul!' There was no answer for a time, and then when Nelson called again, Alison heard Paul walking swiftly into the hall, and from there he called, 'What is it?'

'Can you spare a minute, Mr Paul? There's a gentleman here interested in the long-cased clock. I'd like you to see him.'

Alison sensed Paul's hesitation; then heard him going down the stairs.

As she heard the staircase door close, Alison hesitated for only a moment longer. She couldn't stay in the bathroom indefinitely. She must slip back to bed again, and she would be glad to, for her legs felt like jelly and her heart was racing again. But it was a joyful racing now. Paul wasn't in love with Freda Gordon-Platt, he wasn't, he wasn't. He was in love with her! How stupid she had been. She remembered his high spirits on the afternoon following Mrs Freda Gordon-Platt's visit – she had interpreted his behaviour as pleasure in again seeing the woman he had once loved, when all the time his pleasure had been because he had found release from the bitterness that had eaten into him over the years. And the bitterness was not only because of a lost love and betrayal by a friend, but because of the financial morass the two of them had plunged him into which he was only just now sorting out. Oh, Paul . . . Paul. Poor Paul. Oh, if she could only run to him now and tell him . . . tell him what she had overheard. There would be no more cross-purposes. At this point she thought about the tea-caddy. Oh, the tea-caddy. Well, she could explain that, and he could give it to Miss Beck or to Margaret, whichever he preferred. There was one thing certain; he would not give it to Freda Gordon-Platt.

She crept out of the bathroom and was moving cautiously across the landing when, with a swishing sound, the drawing-room door was pulled open and she was brought to a guilty stop under the eyes of the tall, stiff-faced woman.

'I . . . I understood you were in bed ill.' The voice was cool and high.

'I'm not ill; I have a cold, that's all. I . . . I've just been to the bathroom.' Although the explanation was unnecessary, Alison felt extremely embarrassed at this moment.

Now Freda Gordon-Platt's eyes flashed above Alison's head and across the narrow hall to the bathroom door, and when her gaze returned to Alison she asked, in a deceptively quiet tone, 'May I enquire if you have been in the bathroom long?'

The dislike of this woman rising in Alison again swept away the feeling of embarrassment and she answered provokingly, 'Long enough.'

'Oh.' Mrs Gordon-Platt accompanied this word with an upward lift of her eyebrows and a movement of her head to one side; then turning about she walked back into the drawing-room, saying over her shoulder, 'I would like to have a word with you.'

Alison cast a swift glance towards the stairs. Paul would not be pleased to find her up and talking to this woman, no matter what he himself thought about her. Nevertheless, she followed her into the drawing-room and moved towards the fire.

Freda Gordon-Platt came to a stop a few feet from Alison, standing on the hearthrug, and now she spoke in a quick, low tone, saying, 'Paul may be back in a moment; I want to ask you something.'

'Yes?' Alison turned her head.

'Do you like my son?'

In spite of what Alison knew about this woman's motives, the question came as a surprise. She answered slowly, 'Yes. Yes, I like your son.' This was the truth; she did like Roy.

'Good. Because, as I told you before, he's very much in love with you.'

Alison remained silent for some seconds before saying, 'I can't see how that is possible as we've only met a few times.'

'Time has nothing to do with young people falling in love. You should know that.'

'Roy is only a boy.'

'A boy!' Mrs Gordon-Platt's voice rose now. 'He's the same age as you.'

'He's not. I understand he's not yet twenty and I'm nearly twenty-one.'

'Well, it's a mere point. He's a very sensible boy and he knows what he wants and . . . and he wants to marry you.'

'Really!' Alison looked coldly now at this woman. If

ever there was a schemer, here was one. If she couldn't have Paul for herself she was determined that no-one else was going to have him; moreover, she intended to make him suffer by taking from him the one person who meant something to him.

Alison felt no compunction in playing along with this woman, so she said, 'And you wouldn't mind having me for a daughter-in-law?'

Freda Gordon-Platt shrugged. 'We needn't see each other. Once the house and land are sold' – she didn't say, when Mrs Gordon-Platt is dead – 'Once the house and land are sold, I will leave Roy to his own devices and . . . and his wife. I don't want to hang round his neck nor have him hanging round mine. I have my life before me.' She spoke as if she were still a young girl. Alison turned from her and, taking a comb from the pocket of her dressing-gown, she looked at her reflection in the mirror above the mantelpiece.

She couldn't see Freda Gordon-Platt reflected in the mirror because she was standing out of her vision when she replied, 'I'm afraid I can't marry Roy, Mrs Gordon-Platt, because, you see, I will be marrying Paul at the earliest opportunity.'

She was never clear afterwards as to whether Mrs Gordon-Platt's hands came on her immediately or whether there was a pause before she fell into the fire. Nothing was ever clear about that terrible moment. Only her own screams would return to haunt her again and again in the years that followed.

Paul had always maintained it was dangerous to hang a mirror above the fireplace. He had objected strongly to her doing this; and had often checked her when she stood on the raised hearth so that she could see in the mirror. An impression of these warnings flashed into her mind an instant before she was enveloped in pain, flame and screams.

When she was pushed – or struck – her slippered feet had slipped off the end of the polished hearth and she had fallen forward. The fire was an open iron basket full of glowing coals, and was flanked on both sides by a pair of iron dogs supporting poker and tongs. It was one of those that saved her from falling face first into the basket of flame. Her hands, naturally going forward, struck the hot bars, the left hand to the side, but the right one against the middle of the bars. Then the flames licked and caught her dressing-gown and she was swallowed by it.

'Oh, God! Oh, God!' She was being pummelled now. She let out another piercing scream as she felt herself being rolled in something and almost smothered. Somebody was beating her and this added to her torture. She was rolled again, and now she couldn't get her breath to scream and she was sure she was going to die. She couldn't bear this, she couldn't bear it. Oh, God! Oh, God, let her die. For a fleeting second her whole body went numb. She could feel nothing, nothing. Then she was conscious of sitting on the floor, her head resting against Paul's shoulder, his arms about her. She saw a number of legs; dimly she recognised Nelson's, and Nellie's skirt, and then there were the legs of Freda Gordon-Platt. They were over by the door, and then Paul spoke to them across the room. Alison was conscious of the vibration of his words as they rumbled up from somewhere deep within his body. 'Get out!' he was shouting, 'Get out before I kill you!' Then, 'Get her out of here, Nelson. Get her out ... !' It was at this point that the numbness left her body and she began to groan again and tried not to scream. She clenched her teeth and looked up into the pitying eyes of Paul as he bent above her, murmuring, 'There, my love. There, my love. It won't be long. The ambulance is on its way. It won't be long. There, my love.'

'Oh! Pa-ul.' She groaned out his name and his arms tightened about her.

'My ha ... ands, Paul. Oh! Paul, my hands ... and ... and my face.'

'It's all right. It's all right, my love.' That was all he seemed able to say, 'It's all right, my love.' But it wasn't all right. It wasn't all right. Her face ... her face was burnt. She would look ugly, dreadful, dreadful, like Margaret, poor Margaret. 'Oh, Pa ... ul.' Her body contracted and the pain became unbearable, so unbearable that she was delivered from it and sank thankfully into unconsciousness ... After that, she had a vague recollection of being carried down the stairs; then the pain, mounting once more, blotted everything out again ...

When she next regained consciousness she seemed to be floating in a misty blue light. She called for Paul and one of the figures broke through the mist and brought his face down to hers; but it wasn't Paul's face. This person had a thin nose and bushy eyebrows and he said, 'It's all right. Lie quiet; you'll be all right. The pain will lessen. Just remember that; the pain will lessen.'

Her mind took up the words: The pain will lessen, the pain will lessen. But oh God, it hadn't yet. It was awful, unbearable. If that man could feel this pain, he would know. It would never lessen. She couldn't bear it, she couldn't. Yet she didn't speak. That is not until a woman's voice came in a whisper from somewhere near, saying, 'Tell her about her face.'

Oh, God, her face. Yes, her face. Her face had been burnt. She would look awful, like Margaret, like Margaret. Poor Margaret. Her mind began to race madly; she felt the scream rising in her ... rushing up from the depths of her body. She opened her mouth and her eyes wide, and there was the thin nose and the bushy eyebrows again. 'Listen, you're going to be all right ... There's nothing wrong with your face ...

just smoke, a little singed . . . You understand what I'm saying? Your *face* is all right.' The thin nostrils widened. She watched the lips move into a smile. The eyebrows went up and he said again, 'There's nothing to worry about.'

She wasn't worrying. She wasn't worrying. But oh, the pain, the pain. She didn't care what was the matter with her, not really, if only this pain would stop . . . Oh! the pain.

The female voice was whispering again. 'They never mind so long as it isn't their face, but by heavens, her hands have got it, the right one especially. It'll need some surgery here . . . and her neck . . . Has she drifted off? The injection should be taking effect; she should be easy now.'

Alison clung on to the voice. It was like the voice of God, because, just as it had said, she was becoming easy now. She could bear the dreadful feeling now without shouting inside her head, without screaming against it. They said her hands were in a bad way. And her neck? Oh, she was too tired to think. There was only one thing she knew at this fading moment: she did not care what she looked like so long as the pain didn't return.

Five

IT WAS ONE MORNING ALMOST THREE WEEKS LATER
when Alison, waking up to the familiar sound of
the trolley, saw the white-capped head bending over
her, and smiled at the robust voice that was saying,
'Hello, little-un. Had a good night?'

They all called her 'little-un'. The doctor with the
sharp nose and the bushy eyebrows had started that.
It was only lately that they had, to her, become
individuals, separated from each other by different
clothes and names. Strangely, she felt that she had
always known them, that they had always been with
her, that she had known no other life but the life of
this ward; that she had always lain under this cage and
always been fed by one or other of them, had her hair

combed by them, had been forced to remain alive by them. Only when she saw Paul was she reminded that she had lived another life. Just before visiting hours began, Nurse Riley would tease her in her thick Irish brogue. 'Here comes your great handsome hulk of flesh. My! some folks have it all ways.' It had come to her during the past few days that Nurse Riley – in fact, all of them – were aware of what was between herself and Paul. Yet Paul just sat by the bedside gazing at her, hardly ever speaking. Sometimes he touched her hair. When he left her he kissed her, although not on the mouth. At one stage, when she felt very ill, she had thought dimly . . . I am going to die. I wish he would say it, speak it, say he loved me . . . But he didn't. Yet that night she had been conscious of him being with her all the time, and the next night, too. She was aware now that she had been very ill and had almost died. There was still a great lassitude about her, but when the pain came now it was no longer sharp, but more of a sensation of skin tightening, stretching – cracking, even.

She said to the nurse, 'I've slept well. I feel better.'

'You look better. His nibs will be pleased with you this morning.'

His nibs happened to be the doctor with the thin nose and the bushy eyebrows. Howard by name, and the man who could produce . . . preparation jitters in this tough nurse.

It was a good many hours later when the jitters were in process; the noise outside her own small room had faded away, as if there was no-one left alive in the place, and Alison knew that his nibs was doing his rounds.

Dr Howard was a small man. He moved quickly, he spoke quickly, and he worked quickly. He had no bedside manner. He came breezing in, saying, 'Hello, little-un, how goes it?'

'I feel better, doctor.'

'That's good news. About time too, I think.' He reached out and pulled the chair towards the bed and, leaning towards her, he said, 'We're going to sit up and take notice, aren't we? Have a few visitors and come back to life, eh?'

She tried to nod, and then asked a question that had been niggling at the back of her mind, 'Will my neck be very scarred, doctor?'

'Not when they're finished with it; it'll be like new, better than new.' He touched her cheek now and his voice dropped as he said, 'I'm telling you the truth, you know; not just saying it to placate you. Your neck will be perfectly all right when you've had some treatment.'

'Treatment?' She swallowed. 'How much longer will I be here, doctor?'

'Oh' – he pursed his lips – 'another fortnight, I should think, and then you can go home.'

Her eyes widened. 'Just a fortnight?'

'Yes; and then after a period at home, you'll have to go on to East Grinstead. Now, there's nothing to worry about; nothing will be done until you feel absolutely fit for it, and then only in small doses. It was unfortunate that this should happen at a time when you were on the brink of influenza, which is why you've felt so ill . . . And you *have* been ill.' He patted her cheek again. 'The influenza didn't help the shock either, but now you're going to be all right.'

'My hands, doctor. When am I going to be able to use them?'

'Oh . . . oh.' Again he drew out the word, 'There's nothing much wrong with the left one but your right one has had a pretty bad towsing.'

'I . . . I'll be able to use it?' There was fear in her voice.

'Oh, yes. Yes,' he nodded, 'you'll be able to use it; all, that is, except the little finger. That I'm afraid was damaged pretty badly. But, after all—' he sat up straight and pulled his chin in before saying sharply, 'what is a little finger? Some people lose their hands . . . now don't forget that . . . and their feet. When the loss of use of the little finger troubles you, just remember there's not a mark on your face, and that to me is a miracle. Mr Aylmer caught you only just in time. If it wasn't for his prompt action there is every probability that at least the lower part of your face would have caught it, too. So we're not going to worry about the little finger, are we?'

She smiled a thankful smile, 'No, doctor. And I can go home in a fortnight?'

'There! That's thanks for you.' The chair was pushed roughly back on the polished floor as he bounced round to the sister. 'You do all you can for them and then what happens? They practically insult you by telling you to your face they want to get away from you as soon as possible.' He swung round again to the bed and, his arm stretched to the fullest extent and his finger pointing at Alison, he exclaimed in a voice that one would not associate with a sick room, 'You're an ungrateful hussy. I'm finished . . . I wash my hands of you.' Swinging round he marched out of the room, the sister and the nurse following him, their faces crinkled with subdued laughter.

He was nice. Oh, he was nice. But her finger. She shuddered. Yet, as he had said, it could have been both hands, or her feet, or . . . or her face. She should be thankful. She *was* thankful; and in a fortnight she would be home. Oh, Paul. For the first time in weeks she put pressure on her elbows to change her position in the bed . . .

When Paul came into the room later in the day he stood at the doorway for a moment looking across at her. Then coming slowly towards the bed he smiled at her as he said, 'You're better?'

'I feel fine.' She smiled up at him, and he stood looking down at her for so long that she said, 'Sit down. I've some news.'

When he was settled, and with a touch of excitement that had been lacking in her voice for a long time, she said, 'I'm coming home, Paul.'

'Home? When?' He was leaning towards her, his eyes dark and bright.

'In a fortnight. Dr Howard said so.'

Now the fingers of both his hands were touching her cheeks, and as he beat a gentle tattoo on them she seemed to draw into herself the emotion that was filling him.

'That's splendid. Splendid, splendid . . . I didn't think it would be so soon.'

'I'm going to lose the use of my little finger, Paul.' Her voice was low now and her eyes half veiled.

She watched him place his hands on his knees and look down at them as he said, 'Yes, I know.' Then raising his eyes quickly to hers, he added, 'But that'll be all. Otherwise you'll be as good as new. They do wonderful work at East Grinstead.' But now again his eyes dropped away from hers and he said, 'There's something I must ask you . . . It's about *her*.'

Her . . . could mean only one person, Freda Gordon-Platt. Alison had tried not to think about that person. Even when she was unable to push her aside she remained in a hazy jumble, for she couldn't remember whether the woman had actually pushed her into the fire. But now Paul made things clear. Still looking away from her, he said, 'Time is going on. I'm going to make a case of this. I wanted to know how you felt.'

'A case!' She tried to turn her neck. 'But, Paul . . . against Freda Gordon-Platt?'

'She pushed you into the fire, Alison, deliberately pushed you.'

'But, Paul, I can't remember . . . it's all hazy. Sometimes I think . . . then it all goes hazy.'

'I happened to see her do it.' Paul was looking away now towards the far wall of the room and Alison kept her eyes on him as he went on, 'When Nelson called me to see that customer whom he thought was interested in the William and Mary long-cased clock, I saw at once the man had no intention of buying anything. Nelson should have known this. The man just wanted to know the price and details. He said he had one like it at home, but the clock he described was definitely Georgian. Well, I knew I was wasting my time and I wanted to finish off the business upstairs. But when I opened the staircase door I was surprised to hear your voice and hers too. I went quietly up the stairs and – I make no excuses for myself – I listened.' His fingers came out now and rested against her cheek again, and she closed her eyes as he went on, 'I was near the doorway when you said what you did –' there was a pause as his fingers stroked her cheek and she turned her face just the slightest and pressed against them. 'Then I saw her deliberately push you forward. It all happened so quickly that I was powerless to stop her.' There came another pause, during which she still kept her eyes closed and her cheek pressed firmly against the fingers. Then her eyes sprang open at Paul's next words: 'The following day I asked my solicitors to bring a case against her.'

'Oh, Paul, no. Oh, no.'

'You could have been burnt to death, or anything. It was just a matter of seconds and luck that I was on the spot. Do you know what she nearly did? She nearly killed you.' His face was close to hers now. 'And I feel responsible for it all.'

'No, Paul, no. Don't feel like that. It's over and done with. I provoked her, anyway, and she was under great mental stress. I know she was. I don't like her, I never have . . . You see . . . well' – her eyes remained fast on his – 'I was jealous of her.'

'Oh, Alison.' The words were audible, but only just, for his voice was thick and deep with his pent-up emotion. His face hung above hers, his lips were close and it was at this moment that the door opened and Nurse Riley appeared, saying breezily, 'Oh, I didn't know you had anyone with you. Here's another visitor for you.'

Paul had been about to kiss her, really kiss her for the first time. The moment had been spoiled . . . Oh.

Oh. But when Alison saw Margaret standing hesitantly in the doorway she thrust aside her disappointment, and her smile of welcome was genuine.

Whatever Paul felt was successfully hidden too as he turned towards Margaret, remarking in a surprised tone, 'But I thought you said you wouldn't be able to come.'

'I couldn't when you phoned, Paul, but . . .' Her eyes wavered between Alison and him and then she added, 'Roy came over and offered to look after the children.'

'Oh!' Paul nodded, and following this, the talk became general for a few moments until he said, 'Look, I'll leave you two together. I've got things to see to, but I'll be back in, say, half an hour and pick you up. How is that, Margaret?'

'That would be lovely, Paul. Thanks.'

Paul was bending over Alison now. 'I'll be in this evening.' His head came further down, but his lips only touched her cheek, and then he was gone.

Alison looked up into the scarred face of Margaret. She was not wearing a headscarf today but a hat, and the scars on her face were in full evidence. Alison shuddered inwardly as she looked at them and she sent a prayer heavenwards in thanks for being spared this tragedy.

Looking down at Alison, Margaret said quietly, 'I know how you're feeling and I've been with you in my mind every minute since it happened. I was terrified for you in case your face . . .'

'Oh, Margaret, don't . . .'

'It's all right, my dear, I'm used to it now. It doesn't matter any more, at least, not very much. As long as Robert is alive and I have the children, nothing matters very much. I just live a day at a time now.'

Again Alison said, 'Oh, Margaret!' Without making light of what she herself had gone through, she knew it was nothing compared with what this woman had suffered and was still suffering.

To change the subject, Alison now asked after the children and this brought Roy's name to the fore. 'And you know, Alison' – Margaret was smiling – 'I like that young man very much; he's a good boy.'

'I know. I like him too, Margaret.'

'But you weren't in love with him; not even a little bit?'

'Oh, no, Margaret, not even a little bit.'

Margaret smiled now. 'I tried to soften the blow when I told him about Paul.'

'You told him?'

'I had to, because his mother hadn't. I realised that even after all that had happened she hadn't told him how things stood between you and Paul. I had to tell him in case he came to visit you and met up with Paul and Paul might . . . well . . . I don't want Paul hurt any more.'

'But . . . but Paul knows that there's no-one in the whole world but him.'

'He may know that, Alison, but he's still afraid. Roy's young and attractive.'

'Huh! He's not half . . . no, not a quarter as attractive as Paul.'

'That's how I think, too, but Paul doesn't see it that way. He'll never feel sure of you until you've married him and, being Paul, maybe not even then. You see, the thing that Freda and my brother did to him left him scarred inside. Outside, he looks assured and composed, but inside, like many of us, he doubts himself, he's afraid. You'll have to love him a lot, Alison.'

'Love him a lot! I love him a lot now. Why, I was nearly distracted when I thought he wanted her again.'

Margaret said quietly, 'Has he mentioned anything yet about bringing a case against her?'

'Yes; but it's unthinkable, really, and it would hurt Roy.'

'I'm so glad you think that way; oh, so glad.' Margaret shook her head. 'In a way, you know, I'm sorry for her. I saw her yesterday when I was up at the house.'

'You've been up to see your mother?'

'Yes, several times since you and I last met. She's a changed woman. I took her the tea-caddy and the writing-case . . .'

'Paul gave you the caddy? I . . . I'd forgotten about it. I put it in the wardrobe.'

'Yes, he found it there and brought it to me and I took them both to my mother. It's strange, at least it seems strange to me, that she was more pleased to see me than the caddy or the writing-case, even knowing what was hidden in them, and even stranger still when she gave them back to me on the spot. All she wants now is that I go and see her and take the children with me. She . . . she feels compassion for me. It seems too good to be true, and I feel I'm living in a kind of dream and I'm afraid I'll wake up.'

'Oh, Margaret, I'm so glad for you. And now you need have no more worry. Are you going to buy the smallholding outright?'

'No, no. We're not going to do that. I went to see Robert yesterday and he agreed with me that half of the necklace should go to Roy. That boy has more on his shoulders than he can carry, for now he has to carry his mother.'

'Oh, Margaret, you are so kind. It's yours by right.'

'Nothing is one's own by right. Paul taught me that over his years of self-sacrifice. He taught me that one thing . . . Nothing is yours by right. Because, you know'

– she laughed now – 'if we could be held to that, both what was in the tea-caddy and the writing-case legally belongs to you . . . Do you realise that? It was you who bought both these items – the tea-caddy, I understand, not without a struggle. But nevertheless, if there is any . . . claim, by rights they belong to you.'

'All right.' Alison smiled a mischievous smile, the first that had touched her lips for weeks. 'I'm going to lay my claims to them both. How much do you think they are worth?'

Margaret laughed; then said seriously, 'Paul says the necklace as a whole should bring about fifteen thousand.'

'What!' The movement hurt Alison's neck. 'Fifteen thousand pounds?'

'Yes, perhaps more, he says. He's going up to town next week to place it for auction. It's actually a well-known necklace. The setting is a bit old-fashioned, as it was first made for my great-great-grandmother's attendance at Queen Victoria's Coronation in 1837.'

'And you're going to give half of what it brings to Roy?'

'Well, aren't you giving the whole lot of it back to us? What's the difference? The merit lies with you and not with me. And you can be glad that Roy is having a share, because he's going to put it to good purpose; it will be the making of him. You'll never guess what he intends doing with the money.'

'I can't think.'

'He's going to start building on the estate; on his own land. Instead of selling it to builders for them to erect houses, he's going into the business himself. Of course, in a small way at first, with perhaps just a couple of houses. He's already found a builder who has the experience but no capital, and I think he'll go on from there.'

They talked for a little while longer, and then as Margaret was about to take her leave she said, 'Oh, I musn't forget. Beck sent her' – she paused and moved her head with an exaggeratedly dignified movement – 'deep regard. Those were her own words.'

'Oh, thank her,' said Alison. 'And thank you, Margaret, for coming. You've done me no end of good.'

'You know something?' Margaret was at the door, standing straight, her bearing proud, 'This is the first time for years I've been out alone and without my face covered up. But it won't be the last. Goodbye, my dear. I'll look in again soon.'

'Goodbye, Margaret. Goodbye.'

After Margaret's departure, Alison lay looking towards the door. There was a calmness on her, a waiting calmness, and into it intruded these words of Nelson's, 'Life isn't complete unless you're given a cross to carry.' She didn't want to carry any cross, but wanting or not she had to carry it, not on her shoulders but on her hands and neck. She wasn't finished with pain: there was a weight of it before her, and the pressure of it now frightened her, until she realised that there was a greater pressure in her life, and this pressure tilted the scale heavily downwards – for this pressure was Paul's love.

And this knowledge stayed with Alison during the next two weeks. Also the fact that she would only come to realise it fully when she was back home in her own world at the top of the house in Tally's Rise. For although Paul visited her every day, and sat with her for long stretches at a time, they never again had the opportunity to reach the point that Margaret had interrupted when she paid her first visit.

Then came the day of high excitement, the day when she was to return home. Her farewells had been said, and her thanks given in more than verbal ways. Dr Howard had, in his characteristic way, checked her thanks with, 'No need for goodbyes, for we haven't seen the last of you. Get along now. And be back here a week on Monday, do you hear? for a check up. The nurse will call on you each day. Do what you're told and everything will be all right.'

Paul had spent some time with the doctor before he had come to take her from the ward. His arm was around her shoulders, almost carrying her, and she needed the support, so unsteady were her legs, although she had been getting up for a part of the day for a while now. Then she was in the old familiar car, and as they swung through the hospital gates she settled back against the worn leather and murmured, 'Paul. Oh! Paul. It's wonderful to be alive.'

Paul did not glance in her direction, nor did he even make a comment, and in silence they drove home.

Nelson and Mrs Dickenson were standing behind the shop door waiting, and even before Paul could get Alison out of the car their welcome was pouring over her.

Before she had walked up half the length of the drugget she was crying, and Nelson too, unashamedly, and his voice was thick as he said, 'Aw, lass, this is the happiest day of me life, just to see you back home.'

Slowly, Alison lifted her left arm towards him and he gently patted her sleeve, and would have gone on patting it, but Mrs Dickenson's voice hit him with, 'Now get out of the way; can't you see she's tired? There'll be time enough for you to jabber later. What she wants is a rest and a good meal. And it's all ready, it's all ready.' She went scampering away up the stairs now, as excited as a child.

With Paul's help, Alison took the stairs slowly, one at a time, and as she mounted she murmured again and again, 'Oh, it's wonderful, wonderful to be home.'

On the threshold of the drawing-room she stopped and looked around her, then up at Paul. His eyes were waiting for hers and she leaned her head towards him. He closed the door behind them and led her forward towards the hearth. The fire was burning and she stood for a moment looking down at it: then she looked up above the mantelpiece. The mirror had gone and in its place hung a large oil painting, the whole canvas being taken up with three heads of rhododendron blossom. As she turned from the picture Paul quietly took the coat that hung from her shoulders, and dropping it on the couch, placed his hands gently but firmly on her forearms and drew her towards him. The face that looked down into Alison's now was the face of the Paul she loved, the face of the man who had always made her world. The face of the man she could lean on in the many trials that lay before her. The lips that she was looking at now were trembling slightly. She watched them forming words. Soft and deep they came to her, 'You love me, Alison?'

'Yes, Paul. Oh, yes. I always have, right from the day I first saw you, and I always shall. Always, always.'

A second longer he looked at her, then his lips fell full and hard on hers. There was a breath-checking ecstatic moment before, straining to him, she returned his first real kiss, and as she did so a strange thought entered her mind. It was . . . that only at this very moment was she being born.

ALSO BY CATHERINE COOKSON

THE BONDAGE OF LOVE

Years ago Bill Bailey had met and married Fiona, a young widow with her own family. The Baileys made their home in the Tyneside town of Fellburn, where Bill's business prospered. When one of Fiona's children, Willie, acquired a new friend, the wayward Sammy Love, Sammy and his father Davey were, in various ways, able to enhance the lives and fortunes of the Baileys.

Now with Davey dead there were new challenges to face. It had been agreed that Sammy would live with them — but would this formidable lad with his colourful language fit in as a full-fledged member of the Bailey family? As for Fiona, it was she who bore the brunt of the arguments and disagreements that were an inevitable part of life in the Bailey household. Whatever life had in store, however, she knew she could always rely on Bill, that rock of a man with a rough tongue but a heart of gold.